NIRLIIT

NIRLIIT

Juliana Léveillé-Trudel

TRANSLATED FROM THE FRENCH BY
ANITA ANAND

ESPLANADE BOOKS

THE FICTION IMPRINT AT VÉHICULE PRESS

ESPLANADE BOOKS IS THE FICTION IMPRINT AT VÉHICULE PRESS

Published with the generous assistance of the Canada Council for the Arts, the Canada Book Fund of the Department of Canadian Heritage, and the Société de développement des entreprises culturelles du Québec (SODEC).

We acknowledge the financial support of the Government of Canada through the National Translation Program for Book Publishing, an initiative of the *Roadmap for Canada's Official Languages 2013-2018: Education, Immigration, Communities,* for our translation activities.

SODEC
Québec
Funded by the Government of Canada / Financé par le gouvernement du Canada | Canada

This novel is a work of fiction. Any resemblance to people or events is coincidental and unintended by the author.

Esplanade Books editor : Dimitri Nasrallah
Cover design: David Drummond
Photo of author: Alain Léveillé
Typeset in Minion and Gill by Simon Garamond
Printed by Marquis Printing Inc.

Originally published by Éditions La Peuplade 2015
Copyright © Juliana Léveillé-Trudel and Éditions La Peuplade 2015

English translation copyright © Anita Anand 2018,
Dépôt légal, Library and Archives Canada and
Bibliothèque nationale du Québec, second quarter 2018.

CATALOGUING IN PUBLICATION – See last page

Published by Véhicule Press, Montréal, Québec, Canada
vehiculepress.com

Distribution in Canada by LitDistCo
www.litdistco.ca

Distribution in the U.S. by Independent Publishers Group
www.ipgbook.com

Printed in Canada on FSC certified paper.

FOR MAMAN

*You were right:
it had the makings of a novel*

SALLUIT: SKINNY PEOPLE

KANGIQSUALUJJUAQ: the very large bay
KUUJJUAQ: great river
TASIUJAQ: resembling a lake
AUPALUK: where the ground is red
KANGIRSUK: the bay
QUAQTAQ: intestinal worm
KANGIQSUJUAQ: the large bay
IVUJIVIK: where you are stuck between pieces of moving ice
AKULIVIK: central prong of a harpoon
PUVIRNITUQ: stench of rotten meat
INUKJUAK: resembling a giant
UMIUJAQ: resembling an overturned boat
KUUJJUARAPIK: large pretty river

NUNAVIK: GREAT INHABITED LAND

PART I

EVA

1

IT'S A LONG WAY to your place, Eva. Salluit, sitting on the 62nd parallel, well past the treeline, Salluit, all rolled up in a ball at the foot of the mountains, Salluit, the fjord in the small of the back. Keep going another sixteen kilometres, and you reach the Hudson Strait, which just might bring you to the Arctic Ocean. No one really knows.

There's only one way to get here, by air, and like the geese, *nirliit,* I keep repeating this trip, from north to south and back again, every time summer returns, every time summer ends. First stop, La Grande Rivière, a three-hour flight northwest of Dorval. As the Dash-8 drops under the clouds to fly over the gigantic Robert-Bourassa Reservoir, there is a sudden glimpse of rough and gripping beauty, the reservoir's infinitely dark waters framed by tight rows of pines. La Grande's tiny airport gathers the usual northern wildlife. Geologists from the Department of Natural Resources. Nurses. Social workers. Me. I'm not really sure which category I belong in. Strangers who would never talk to each other back in the city strike up animated conversations here; they burst out laughing. White people: *Qallunaat.* The Inuit don't talk. Not to us. We don't talk to them either. The whites in one corner, Inuit in the other. "Whites" also means blacks. Anyone who is not Inuit is white here. I'm sure Martin Luther King would have been tickled.

Next stop: Puvirnituq, "stench of rotten meat." I rename all the movies and songs I think of: "Stench of Rotten Meat, Mon Amour," " It's Raining Roses on Stench of Rotten Meat," "Midnight in Stench of Rotten Meat". Puvirnituq, the Bronx of the North, Puvirnituq of the conspiratorial whispers and smiles, P.O.V.—Puvirnituq. It's not much of a postcard paradise, nothing like Kangiqsujuaq or Salluit, the queens of northern beauty. No splendid mountain or dizzying cliff, just a flat plain broken here and there by a small hill. A miserable little place, where crime can thrive, a place that wins the title of Most Violent Community in Nunavik year after year. Nothing here that would normally make you feel like lingering. And yet, you really ought to. Puvirnituq is a plain girl with magnificent eyes that you only discover if you're paying attention. You have to see the river, how gorgeously it snakes its way around the tundra before flowing into Hudson Bay at the northernmost point of the village. The meeting of the river and the ocean is the most beautiful place for kilometres. But you have to keep your eyes on the water, you can't let them slide over to the side; otherwise, they'll fall on that other river: the river of garbage, the municipal dump that displays its metal and plastic treasures as if attempting to compete with the splendours of nature. My eyes can't stop going from one river to the other, can't tear themselves away from this stark picture of what we've done to the country.

Salluit at the end of the road, only the geese keep pushing north. Pointlessly, I search out your face in the airport. I so wish I could hear your husky voice saying *welcome back*, these two words that have always been enough to reassure me that coming back was the right thing to do. *Tunngasugit Salluni*: Welcome to Salluit. You taught me how to say that last year. You taught me how to say all kinds of things in your language of rugged poetry; you patiently repeated those words for me. Me, a child struggling to articulate the syllables of this bewildering language, with its many q's, k's and j's. You were so sweet and patient as you encouraged my laboured efforts; each properly assimilated word lit up your face with that radiant smile, *aliana*: "I am happy."

And yet, it's true that we don't understand each other very well. Your broken English and practically nonexistent French drive white people crazy, yet who among us has seriously given your language a try? Who can talk to you in Agaguk's language? Who bothers wrangling with the q's, k's and j's to understand and speak the language of the tundra? Who? How can we blame someone for not mastering our language when we can't say anything in theirs? Your language, which is increasingly streaked with English words, hasn't kept up with technology, can't even say *computer*. Your language, in which the young struggle to connect with the old, which has fallen under the spell of Justin Bieber and Rihanna, and which is melting away at about the same rate as the permafrost.

You aren't there in the big crowd pressing up against the fence in front of the landing strip. Three days in the fog, three days without a plane, three days cut off from the rest of the world; you're not there but a chorus of *welcome backs* rings out all the same from all over the place. I pop out of the plane like a toy from a cereal box, and five seconds later the children are running at me, straight at my belly, squeezing me like little boa constrictors. It's good to be home.

2

Lizzie tells me about it; Lizzie, your co-worker who used to see you every morning for, I don't know, maybe five years, maybe less?

You people, you change jobs pretty often.

I hate all those *you peoples:* "you people, you *white* people." I've heard that so many times and each time I've felt like just taking off. I've been so tempted to just leave the person standing there alone with those words, "you people". I am not "you people" and yet, look, I say it too, I just did. "You people, you Inuit. You people, you Inuit, you change jobs pretty often."

I just said it, Eva, and you probably understand what I really meant, basically something like: you can't keep a fucking job, you never manage to go in every morning, to go to bed sober the night before, to actually get up at a decent hour. I'm sorry. I don't really mean it, not that much, not anymore. It's just that I'm sure that most of us white people are not really thrilled about going to work in the morning either, you know; it's just that we force ourselves to, we trample those longings down, and we do it. But there are hundreds of thousands of us who feel just like you; damn, I'd rather go caribou hunting right now, please bring me to the tundra, oh, please, get me out of here. What if I said I was sick this morning, or my kid was sick, or my car broke down this morning or what if I said—but no, it's no good, it's not right. The difference with you people is that you don't try to hide behind excuses. You say: I was drunk, I was sleeping, I went hunting.

Lizzie, your co-worker, the one who saw you every morning for, I don't know, maybe five years, tells me the story in this cold, almost detached voice. He threw your body in the water, your fragile little body into the dark, rocky waters of the Hudson Strait. Oh, Eva, your body, all the way down at the bottom now, gone to join those of the fishermen who ended their lives beneath the waves because you people, you Inuit, you never wear life vests. You say yes to death even before it comes calling because for thousands of years life has been like this, so unforgiving; January's cold, so cold that it burns; all those cruel, dark days with only five hours of sunlight, and anyway, where could a fisherman be happier than in the water?

Your body's down in the water and your spirit is everywhere, out on the surface of the sea, in the tundra, in the never-darkening sky of the Arctic summer. It's dancing. Oh, Eva, yes, dance! I'm saying your words now, the way you would in your broken French: "You miss to me."

Lizzie says they haven't found your body, the one that sat all those years on that chair that I see from the corner of my eye; your body, which held your head and your smiling face at the Northern Village of Salluit reception desk; your body behind the welcome desk; your body the first thing we saw upon entering, and your eyes and your smile. *You miss to me.*

Lizzy says, "No, no ceremony, at least not this month. The priest isn't here. He won't be back before August, so no ceremony." And I hear her thinking no *body*, no ceremony, I hear the dozens of Jesuses displayed around her office shouting no body, no ceremony. I am so fed up with her compassion for poor, suffering Jesus; I want to yell that we mortals suffer too, Christ! And then I remember: it happened to Lizzie too. No body for her husband, no body for her son-in-law, nor for her son-in-law's father. All three of them at the bottom of the fjord too; it's been two years now. That was my first summer; that's right, another summer when I arrived right after death. Three fishermen in a canoe. Only the boat came back.

God, look at you all, with lives like Greek tragedies. How you would make Shakespeare drool with your horrible pain and despair! I have no idea how you cope. I have enough trouble dealing with my own little problems.

3

WE ARE THE NEW WHITE missionaries. We preach healthy living. Don't smoke, don't drink, don't take drugs, don't eat fast food, eat more fruit and veggies, get eight hours of sleep every night, go to bed early, exercise, don't skip school or work, don't litter, slow down when you're driving your quads, wear a life vest when you're in your boats, keep your firearms out of the reach of children, practice safe sex, don't swear, say please and thank you when you ask for something, vaccinate your children and sterilize your dogs. You must find us incredibly irritating.

Wednesday night at the Co-op. Chips, Pepsi, cigarettes: the essential elements of the Inuit diet. You can get them at two places in town: the Co-op, managed by Inuit, and the Northern Store, run by white people. The same products, in general, same crazy high prices, but with completely opposite vibes. A cheerful, unholy Inuit mess versus the irreproachable orderliness of the *Qallunaat*. You wait ages to get to the till at the Co-op, versus a couple of minutes at the Northern. You choose the shortest line even though you know that it will end up being the slowest. Even when you strategically choose to stand behind the Inuk with only a few items to buy, they always manage to surprise you once they get to the cash register.

13 Cokes. 9 Pepsis. 1 pack of cigarettes. 3 lollipops. 2 jawbreakers and 6 Mr. Freezies. 4 Jos Louis'. 1 pack of salt and vinegar chips. Taima. (That's everything.) Oh no, I forgot the milk, I'll be right back. Oops, I don't have enough money. Uh, all right, take away two of the Cokes. No, three of the Cokes. Okay. Taima.

And everything is so expensive. There's hardly anything to buy; in fact, there's fuck all, but everything costs so much. Mushy vegetables, banged-up fruit, a head of lettuce frozen here and there from its time in the refrigerated hold of an Air Inuit plane. Even an old loaf of bread, its first few slices covered in mould, costs a fortune. You notice it afterwards, but you don't go back to the store to exchange it because that's just the way it is. A fortune for food items hardly acceptable for a clearance sale in the South. And sometimes the plane doesn't even come. Sometimes the weather is just too awful. Sometimes there isn't any more bread, or milk, or anything. Sometimes, like a country at war, the store is empty, and when the plane comes back, we are glad to see our wilted vegetables and brownish fruit again.

The only thing that is never lacking is frozen pizza, and yet God knows you eat enough of it! Eva, I never invited you over for supper. I wish I could invite you over now. Why are we so shy to invite each other over? You never set foot inside my house. My *big* house, well, no, it's not that big, but it is big considering it's just me here by myself. A house like that can easily accommodate ten people, yet I live alone and I have a big house. They told me not to let the kids inside; they said it would never end. "If you say yes once, it's over." They told me to be firm. The other white people told me that. So I listened to them, and when kids knock on my door and ask for apples, I give them some, but outside on the porch. I feed them the way you feed kittens, not inside the house. They told me not to let them in.

Eva, do you want to come in my house?

.

The kids follow me down the street. They want to go where I go. They squeeze me like bears. They watch me closely. Very closely.

They touch my nose.

It's so big!

Not that big. We white people have big noses. Mine isn't much better or worse than anyone else's.

They touch my belly.

Do you have a baby?

No, and I am not fat. Women my age already have three kids. I don't even have one yet. You wonder when I'm going to get started.

They touch my legs.

You shave your legs?

Yes. We white people, we're hairy.

You find that funny.

They explore my body like kittens. Everything that is different about me amuses them. They stare deeply into my eyes, amazed at how blue my irises are. They touch my hair. They look through the sleeves of my t-shirt, searching for the hair in my armpits. They snuggle like kittens seeking warmth, wanting to be petted.

4

ARCTIC SUMMER. There is no night, ever. The sun disappears behind the mountains, splashing the clouds with an orange light. It disappears, but doesn't set. It's dark, but never black. Good luck trying to explain that to people in the South. Try explaining the exact amount of light, the effect it has, the colour of the sky. Tell them that it depends; it depends on whether or not it was sunny during the day, as sunny days make lighter nights, grey days make greyer nights—the night, the cats, everything grey. Tell them it's as though it was 9 p.m. on a July evening, yeah, that's it, 9 p.m. in July. Everything is grey or silver, the fjord is silver; tell them that when the fjord is silver, it's so beautiful that it makes you want to cry. I often feel like crying, even if I'm not sad. It's just that everything is too much here, too beautiful or too harsh.

Are you sleeping? How on earth do they manage to sleep?

They don't sleep. The kids gallop around the village all night; they play kids' games, and sometimes other games. Sometimes they steal gas from the sheds and spray everything they find and set fire to it, and they add more gas so that the blaze gets bigger and when there isn't any more they go back and try to find some at someone else's place. Quads, snowmobiles and boats all need a lot of gasoline, so there is plenty to be found everywhere. Sometimes I think they are really going to set fire to something huge, something like a house. Sometimes I think they're going to burn themselves, they're going to destroy themselves, but they know what they're doing. They've been walking the line between life and death for so long, and with such irreverence, that they're invincible.

It's as they get older that things start getting out of control, when the little fires aren't enough anymore, or even the shacks and houses. There was the son of Qumaaluk, your other co-worker, who emptied a gallon of gasoline on himself one fall, almost two years ago now. Up in smoke at the age of twenty-two, gone to fatten those alarming statistics of abject distress, the ones that are exploding under the weight of hundreds of indigenous people who leave us every year with a resounding *fuck off*. Qumaaluk's son set himself on fire in the shack. She told me herself at the airport. Even before leaving Montreal, these boreal tragedies already roaring in my ear. When we see someone after a long time, we have to be prepared for anything. There is no way we can just ask "How are you?"—an absurdly banal question to which you don't really expect an answer. "How are you?" here, could result in an answer like, "Not very well, my son set himself on fire last fall." Qumaaluk says that we're all going to die, but still, it shouldn't happen like that; Qumaaluk says she can't accept her son's death. Qumaaluk is up and about and is taking care of her two other kids who aren't five years old yet and who are as blond as wheat, something they got from their Qallunaaq dad. A whim of genetics: they have Inuit faces and the blondness of the South. Qumaaluk is surrounded by angels, and it's lucky she is because there are too many deaths to count here.

.

And you, Eva, you've gone to join those other statistics, the ones where you are overrepresented, those of women who are victims of violence. Not conjugal violence, although it could have been. There's quite a bit of violent love here between the walls of these mostly identical houses; there's fierce jealousy, there's the confusion between love and possession, you who possess so much but so little.

Your house doesn't belong to you. Neither does your land. All of that is graciously lent to you by the government. Isn't that nice of us? We steal your land, but we let you borrow it back afterwards. Is that why you have such a strong need to possess stuff? Snowmobiles, boats, quads, trucks taking up all three blocks of the village, all to escape your overpopulated houses, where you live piled on top of each other. Somehow, you lack space in this huge northern expanse. How is it that all of this abundance looks so much like the Third World?

The construction guys are jealous. *I fucking wish I could afford a Ski-Doo and a boat; I wish I didn't have to fucking work and could just spend all my days fishing, Christ, they have it good.* I've heard it before, in the South as well; a lot of people wish they could trade places with the welfare bums.

It rains money on you here, but it dries up as well, as soon as it comes, in fact, precisely because they've introduced you to all kinds of expensive stuff to keep you entertained and distracted. Right, Eva? Do you remember your old boyfriend, the school principal? Do you remember that wonderful family man who used to keep you supplied with booze whenever he wanted sex? Booze costs a fortune here, but then again, everything does, even a pint of milk, so nobody balks at the fact that a ten-ounce bottle of vodka will set you back two hundred dollars. The school principal didn't have to pay that much. For us white people, it's easy enough to bring booze up from the South, bring up a lot and give it out as we wish. One blowjob for one ten-ouncer: it's the law of supply and demand.

·

Did anyone ever tell you that your eyes were stunning, and your smile as well?

This place is dangerous for beautiful women. Nancy runs to meet me: that chubby, sullen preteen is turning into a ravishing young teenager. So lovely with her hair up, wearing her long earrings, her body stretching tall and slender, her big eyes outlined with makeup. Her thirteen years look so good on her, and on her pretty friends as well, and I wonder how much longer, how much time do you have left? How long before your too-pushy boyfriend forces your first time on you, if it hasn't already happened, how long before you get pregnant and never dare consider having an abortion? Abortion doesn't happen here, not even for a thirteen-year-old kid, not even for a victim of rape or incest.

Well Eva, *you* know: a grandmother at forty, your son Elijah and the lovely Maata, the lovely and tiny Maata, sixteen years old and a baby in the hood of her parka; sixteen years old and a cashier at the Co-op, baby in the pram parked next to the cash register, but oh, how proud you were. You Inuit really love children more than anything in the world. Even though you often don't love them well enough, you still love them.

How long will it be before the harshness of this northern lifestyle completely ravages this dazzling beauty of yours? How long before a series of pregnancies and a series of Cokes, consumed the way a chain-smoker goes through cigarettes, make you gain about fifty pounds? How long before booze, cigarettes and sleepless nights prematurely wrinkle your lovely faces, and the dozens of kinds of candy available at the Co-op ruin most of your teeth? How long before you're twenty-five years old but look forty? Sometimes it's not very long; sometimes you reach the summit of your beauty at thirteen and it's over by fourteen. Sometimes you're too hard on yourselves or else it's life that isn't kind. Sometimes, by fourteen, those pretty Northern roses have already wilted.

There's Julia, a stunning beauty last summer, a future queen, but it's over now, her features bloated and distorted by booze and drugs, her body heavy with all the garbage that the Co-op sells cheaper than vegetables, the light in her eyes taken away by I don't know what sadness—oh, Julia. Julia drags her feet heavily through the streets of Salluit. She quit school and does nothing with her days but walk around with her hopelessness, her renunciation of the world, sometimes alone, sometimes with other people who share the same misery. Our paths often cross, and the little girls who follow me around whisper in my ear, pointing: *The drop-outs*. They might as well be saying: *They have the plague*, or *They have AIDS*. It's the same tone of voice, the tone of disaster, the tone of shame and contempt. And yet you too, my poor little darlings, you're probably going to end up like them because your school has no idea how to keep you within its walls.

5

A GOOD NUMBER of white people have tasted the salt of your skin, and this allows them to forget their jealousy and your Ski-Doos. They forgive you for all that free money you receive as they invade and possess your daughters. The younger they are, the more attractive. The police can't do anything about it because they too, succumb. Right, Mathieu, new recruit of the Kativik Regional Police? Mathieu and Aida, barely eighteen. Aida, the most beautiful girl in Salluit, the village's greatest hope, accepted at Marie Victorin College. Aida will be leaving at the end of the summer. Aida, please don't fall in love. I don't mean to insult your intelligence or your charm, but often twenty-seven-year-old men who fall for girls your age, well, I'm just saying: you could do better.

Sometimes it's the opposite, sometimes it's the girls here who absolutely want to taste the skin of the guys who come here from the South, girls who want blue-eyed babies, girls who name their children Sébastien or Patrick to remember the Sébastien or Patrick who came up North for a little while to work on a few houses and make a few kids. These girls prowl around the hotel and the work camps. Antoine is terrorized, barricaded in a hotel room that goes for two-hundred-and-fifty dollars a night, Antoine the architect with eyes the kind of blue you've only ever seen on huskies. The girls lining up in front of his hotel would knock on his door if they were allowed to come in. But Antoine thinks of his girlfriend back in Quebec City.

Gaétan doesn't really think about his wife back in Boucherville, but the old engineer is no longer of an age to be making children. He returns from work every night without tasting the exotic beauty of the northern girls; there is no line of girls waiting for him in front of his house. He still loves to hear about the conquests of his young workmates, and to hold forth on questions of genetics.

It's good for them, you know. The more white mixing in with Inuit blood, the more they improve. I've noticed some improvement already.

Gaétan bows low to these great young gods of the construction sites: thank you for spreading your seed far and wide for the improvement of the race, thank you for passing on your precious blood to the many children you will never bother meeting. Don't worry about whether or not their mothers have the means to buy milk and diapers. As long as they possess your wonderful genetic baggage, it's all fine.

Saturday morning at the Co-op, Saana and Maggie lingering

in the baby food aisle. Saana frowns at the label on the little jar she's holding, Maggie busy with her bottle, just *criminally* adorable. Maggie in my arms now. Inuit babies are so warm, built to withstand the harsh cold. A bit of joy on a Saturday morning. Sébastien or Patrick thousands of kilometres away, missing it all. Sébastien or Patrick won't ever see this bustling, child-filled tundra anymore. Well, too bad, it's their loss.

6

SATURDAY AFTERNOON, mild wind on the tundra. A mother ptarmigan and her little ones scatter in panic as I approach. They don't know that I only want to admire their beauty. The mother wants to protect her chicks, but really, how can a ptarmigan protect itself? No teeth, no claws, the chicks can't even fly. This is life in all its magnificence and fragility. A flower on the tundra. It makes me want to cry. I've said it before: I often feel like crying here because everything is too beautiful or too hard. I see a ptarmigan on the mountain and I want to cry. Meanwhile, in the village: children and violence.

I believe you would have spared the bird because otherwise the little ones would have died, and you understand the importance of species renewal. You love animals, but not exactly like us; you love them because they have fed and clothed you for thousands of years. You've never been afforded the luxury of being vegetarians, like me. I'm a vegetarian and you ask what that is, with the same intonation as all Inuit when they speak French, "C'est quoi ça?" It's impossible to be a vegetarian here, and I've cheated. I adore caribou. Nobody would eat tofu after having tasted caribou. Just try to explain that to the others, down there, to describe the taste; but actually, it's simple: it tastes like the tundra.

You feel I wander too far away by myself, you say it's dangerous, you say but the wolves, *amaruit,* you say not to leave without a gun. I say that I'm more dangerous with one than without one, and you laugh. I love it when you laugh.

Everyone knows someone who hasn't returned. Everyone knows someone who was taken away by the fog. Everyone has lost a friend or a member of his family in the blizzard. Everyone knows the story about the nurse from Kangiqsujuaq, and everyone knows the three hunters, found four days later or the following spring. The polar cold like a shroud; it preserves a body well, just to taunt us.

You humbly accept the fury of the elements, but sometimes no, sometimes you revolt against the harsh injustice. Sometimes a murderous avalanche starts early in the morning on New Year's Day, buries the school where the whole village had come together to celebrate, and your cries of pain resonate deep in the tundra: Kangiqsualujjuaq, in 1999.

7

JULY IN A COTTAGE somewhere near the bottom of the bay. A cottage is a heap of old plywood, bits of sheet metal, leftover insulation meticulously piled on top of each other to create these shacks scattered around the tundra, these little oases of tranquility which you escape to as often as you can, especially during the summer. A cottage somewhere near the bottom of the bay, an Inuk woman about, I don't know, sixty-three or one-hundred-and-thirteen years old. A bad smell catches your throat before you've even come through the door. Someone's dead, an old person has been forgotten and left to die, another drama. But no, actually, the only thing that's dead is this enormous beluga, and the old lady is cooking up its skin. Mountains of carefully removed fat marinate in pots. In a week this precious liquid will be transferred into large containers, which will in turn be crammed into the communal freezer. Some evenings the whole village will come and dip their pieces of frozen caribou in it: Inuit champagne. You adore that too, Eva, I know. I would have had some in your honour, but the smell of a corpse is too much for me.

Do you remember when I plucked a ptarmigan? On all fours on old pieces of cardboard to protect the floors, the bird killed the winter before, just taken out of the freezer, its feathers white and immaculate; but not for long, the blood spraying under the knife, the skin that comes off in one piece, like a banana peel. You know white people buy their meat at supermarkets, where everything is clean, there are no feathers, no little hairs, and especially no blood, nothing to remind us that this thing wrapped in Styrofoam was running around and making noise just a few days before. On all fours across old pieces of cardboard, a beautiful beast, frozen forever in its white beauty, and I stick my knife into its virginal purity. You were proud of me; you asked if I had eaten its heart. Your people eat the whole heart raw, all in one go, but I can't, Eva. It's like with beluga fat or putrefied walrus. Sometimes—it's rare, but it happens—a hunter brings back a walrus and you leave the whole enormous animal to rot for days on the beach. Then the families come, one at a time, and they each cut off a piece. The entire village stinks, for days. The smell is just horrible. And when everyone has had his share, the bears come and finish off what's left.

8

Raglan Money Day. Christmas in July. The most awaited moment of the year, when Glencore gives the village back some of the profits from the Raglan mine, which is located on Salluit land. And then it's raining money, rivers of dollars eroding the tundra. Over here, ladies and gentlemen, there's enough for everyone. Everyone come get your precious cheque. Everyone, yes, everyone, from infants to old people, women and children first. This demented frenzy takes over the whole village, wolves fighting over a fresh caribou carcass.

Lauren, the exhausted Manitoban in charge of the Northern Store, has been dreading this day for weeks. Her many wrinkles attest to the ten hard years she has spent here. She's the business missionary, sacrificed like so many others on the altar of the Northwest Company. Lauren tells me about the village as it used to be, before the generous cheques (stamped Glencore), when there were ten or so cars driving around Salluit's four blocks: one for the Northern, another for the Co-op, one for the hotel. For Air Inuit, the police, the school and for the city. Lauren tells me about a place where drugs and alcohol existed but were not consumed to the same degree, where violence did not happen as frequently, and where people took pride in their work. Lauren is from Manitoba. She hasn't heard of Félix Leclerc. I translate his words for her: "The best way to kill a man is to pay him to do nothing."

Lauren gives me a sad smile and nods before going back to her war preparations. Tonight the whole village will invade her store, a giant mob at her counter pushing and shoving to cash their long-awaited cheques. They'll take their beautiful wad of cash and lovingly caress it before stashing it away somewhere in their house. They'll plunge their hands into the pile with joy, fling the banknotes in the air and watch them fly around, and if they're lucky, will sleep on them in a drunken stupor, will not have the energy to drive their brand new SUV into a telephone pole or get into a fight with members of their family. Tonight and for several days, Salluit will be a place of outlaws like the Far West, until all this treasure has melted away like the Arctic ice floe. It won't be long, Lauren knows. They can burn thousands of dollars in no time: in less than a week, the emergency aid coupons given out by the Kativik regional government will once more be traded for food, whereas two days earlier, televisions and computers were being bought by the dozens.

I wonder if Isaakie will be back this year. Isaakie of Ivujivik, the neighbouring village that has no share in this mining manna. Last year, they sent for him to help out on the Raglan Money Day weekend. Who is this Isaakie? He's just the guy who drives the sanitation trucks to Ivujivik. It's a job that has to be done in each of Nunavik's fourteen communities. Some trucks have to supply houses with water and others have to dispose of sewage. Or, to put it poetically, there's a water tank and a shit tank. Isaakie spent the Raglan Money Day weekend picking up the shit of the Sallumiut, who were too busy celebrating their sudden wealth to take care of it themselves. He worked like a madman, alone in his huge truck, to service the whole village. Of course he won't receive a cent of Raglan money, but he has seen everything: the booze, cars, drugs, televisions, Ski-Doos, the huge piles of banknotes, whatever. I wonder if Isaakie felt like leaving them there in their shit while they danced their money dance right in front of him, while they were the kings of the world and him just a poor jerk from outside their circle. I doubt if Isaakie feels like coming back this year.

They're starting to resent you in the other villages, aren't they, Eva? Don't we hear more and more stories about those Salluit people who think they're pretty special, think they're pretty hot seal shit. Some voices are starting to get louder, voices asking why the money isn't being shared amongst all of Nunavik's communities, since the land doesn't just belong to Salluit people, but to all Inuit. I still love everyone here, Eva, with the same possessive kind of love as yours. Salluit is my village. It takes so little to feel biased. I feel like a broken-hearted mother hearing about the awful things her kids have done. I often defend you, but sometimes I get like Lauren, the exhausted Manitoban, and I just nod with a sad smile.

Lauren isn't the only one bracing for the worst tonight. There are also the nurses, the police, and the social workers, all of them aware that parties often turn bad here. If we were cynical, we could place bets: how many casualties will be picked up by a Medivac and flown to the hospital in Puvirnituq—*Stench of Rotten Meat, Mon Amour*? How many brawlers will fill the tiny village prison? How many vehicles will end up in the ditch on their very first ride? But the *how much* that interests you is how much you are going to get this year, how much, oh, how much, more or less than last year? You won't get your share this year, Eva. I wonder what you would have done with it. Among all the questions I never thought to ask you, I never asked what you did with your nickel money. We white people don't dare talk to you about the money that emerges from the depths of that mine because we know it might seem like jealousy, contempt or covetousness. And sure, there are plenty of white people who are filled with jealousy, contempt and covetousness. But not me, Eva, I swear. Not me.

9

WE TAKE TO SEA ABOARD the F/V *Tallurunnaq*, old Tiivii at the stern, poised and calm, squinting as he examines the horizon. Three hours to Deception Bay, which couldn't be more perfect. A cloudless sky and a silky sea, smooth as a mirror. A few caribou on the mountains, a seal or two under the waves, and you. And you? As we leave the fjord for the Hudson Strait my rib cage cracks open to let in the North wind. Heading off into open sea in the Arctic can open you up from the inside. The wind gets under my coat and makes it billow; I'm puffy, blown up, like some inflatable thing. I wish I could just keep pushing on up to the Northwest Passage. On the deck of the F/V *Tallurunnaq* I dream of the *Amundsen*. Tiivii doesn't know what time we'll be back.

You white people, you're so obsessed by time.

I hate hearing *you white people*, but I like Tiivii. Tiivii and his many descendants, his wisdom, the way he brings back scallops for the whole village when he goes fishing. He's good for me, he distracts me from the dark water that I can't stop myself from staring into, trying to find you. There were rumours, you know, when you left. All kinds of rumours. Some were nice, like the one about you being far away with a rich and handsome lover who convinced you to leave everything behind for him. And some that were not so nice, stories of knives and white guys, a *bunch* of white guys, who skinned you like a dirty seal. Human beings are the same everywhere: we'd rather believe the culprit isn't one of us, one of our own. The investigators searched underneath houses, in freezers. They asked tons of questions. They were sent here just for you, you know, like in the movies. The women were scared; they didn't want to go out alone anymore, as if a hungry, preying wolf was loose in the village. It was awful.

I can't find you, not in the fjord, nor in the strait, nor in the bay, and we end up coming back, I don't know at what time, it's not important. Tiivii and I on the deck of the F/V *Tallurunnaq*. Tiivii was born in an igloo. He saw his brothers and sisters die at a time when only the strongest could survive. He hugs his grandson, who plays on his iPhone. Tiivii asks if I have lost something in the water. Yes, as it happens, a beautiful woman around five-foot-three, a hundred and twenty pounds. But I don't say anything.

10

SOMETIMES WE FEEL GOOD here, and safe too. We can be alone and at peace at the edge of a magnificent fjord. We are far from the bustle of a big city, and when we climb to the top of any one of the surrounding mountains, we can take in the whole village at once. We can mentally trace the road from the bottom of the bay all the way to the strait, see the sky burst into a thousand colours as the sun begins to go down behind the cliffs.

Beauty in the form of a punch to the gut: only the tundra has this, an immense, shattering landscape, so lonely with almost no one to appreciate it.

Sometimes we forget about everything else. We're completely consumed by the North wind. We listen to the news from the city, which never has anything to say about us and which takes place so far away, in another country, and we care as little as they care about us. When the fog covers the houses and the planes don't land for days, the rest of the world ceases to exist and there is only us, here, alone.

But sometimes, too, the North is connected to the rest of the world. For most of us white peole, the North is encoded in our DNA like a remote link in our blood, which also contains the blood of the First Nations. Remember your great-great-great grandmothers, you young ones.

We live dispersed across this huge continent, in cities and villages with pretty names that Europeans find enchanting, pretty names that we are eager to translate because we are so proud to know that Quebec means "where the river narrows" in Algonquin, that Canada means "village" in Iroquois or that Tadoussac comes from Innu and means "teats." And, of course, there are all these lovely words in the dictionary, like toboggan, kayak and caribou. There was a time when generations of men born to small farmers heard the call of the forest and ran to join the *savages*. There was a time when we were very close; we were intimately connected. But, alas, it's over now and we have such a short memory. We don't remember anything anymore, and in the cities where towering concrete hides the sun, busy people walk, rarely looking at one another, on roads that split the forest—and once in awhile, their eyes fall on *them*. *Those* people, those human wretches soaked in alcohol who represent not even a shadow of the proud hunters they used to be. *Those* people, whose great talents no longer have a place in our overwhelming new world, who were massacred almost out of existence by one or another of those pieces of shit who, it would appear, always play a major role in "civilization." *Those* people, like a shameful disease, a bad feeling that greets you at the edge of the sidewalk, a problem child who disgraces his parents. They have left their reserve or their village, have somehow ended up on the cement paths of Montreal, Winnipeg or Vancouver. Now they reassure the busy passersby by confirming their prejudices: drunks, layabouts, irresponsible bums.

Suddenly, they land in Charline's field of vision. Charline is a fifty-four-year-old secretary whose prejudice is carefully maintained, like the cedar hedge in front of her house in Sainte Julie. Fifty-four years of bad dye jobs, tanning salons and soap operas. Fifty-four years old, in all her fat, outraged taxpayer splendour, sick to her stomach of all the politically correct bullshit.

They aren't easy on the eyes, are they?

And you, Charline, how are you doing, sweetheart?

11

EIGHT O'CLOCK on a Sunday morning. Four girls, drunk at eight on a Sunday morning in a black Mazda. Four girls miraculously unhurt despite the many times their car has rolled over. Four girls laughing as they extricate themselves from what remains of the vehicle. One of them comes toward me, saying, "Don't call the ambulance, I'm the ambulance!"

A few months earlier, the Kativik police stopped one of the white guys on the construction crew who was driving his truck with a slightly higher alcohol level than what is allowed by law. He lost his driver's license. But at least he had one, unlike most of the people who live here.

The black Mazda will end up in the vehicle cemetery, an open field behind the police station crammed mostly with almost-new four-wheelers, Ski-Doos and cars, all reduced to immobility. All of this is blamed on the snow, the ice, blizzards, wind, the sharp curve on the way to the airport, the dangerous hill on the road beside the river. Or else it's blamed on quarrelling couples, like Mark and Vicky. After a shouting match with his girlfriend, Mark got into his quad and sped off, intending to lose himself in the tundra, find a quiet corner to finish off his last bottle, shoot at a few rocks to keep himself from raising a hand against her, or against their daughters. But it's over now. Mark and his quad are each sleeping in their respective cemeteries. I didn't know. I ran into Vicky and just asked her how things were going. "Not so good, my boyfriend killed himself driving his quad last fall. My oldest daughter hasn't gotten over it. She's only ten but she's already skipping classes. I think she's started taking drugs. Christ, you know, fall is so rough."

A Jeep with a broken window, covered in plastic wrap, driven by a woman, a baby on her knees and a cigarette in the corner of her mouth. A scooter helmed by an old lady, at least eighty-five, two kids between her arms and the handlebars, another one in the back. An all-terrain vehicle carrying eight people plus provisions, driving toward the tundra. Teenage girls driving around the village all day and all night. The backseat of a van serving as a piece of garden furniture. Snowmobiles, tons of them, waiting for winter, or for death. A proposed bylaw to prohibit joyriding after midnight. Lizzie doesn't understand why I find that funny. I can't explain it to her. Not with her office chock full of Jesuses staring at me. Alex, who is teaching me how to drive like an Inuk, jumps over rocks bigger than both of us, like an invincible monster truck. A treacherous mud puddle splashes us up to our thighs. The old Honda, camouflaged like a wild beast deep in mud, refuses to start. Alex and I are brown from head to toe like an ad for Tide. We return on foot.

Sun and twenty incredible degrees. It happens once a summer. All the village big shots whiz around and around on their new vehicles, the sleeves of their t-shirts rolled up. The others, overwhelmed by the heat, bury themselves in the shade of their homes. I slip on my bathing suit and jump into the water with the kids, who can't believe this is happening. The heat wave is like a herd of caribou: when it comes by, you leave everything and follow it.

12

ELISAPIE SLIPS her hand into mine.

Where is your village?

She speaks softly. From the top of a hill we contemplate hers. We can see the whole place in one glance. I don't feel like talking about the big city where I live though I have been there for eight years now. Instead, I tell her about the place where I grew up, Kingsbury, which is no more like Salluit than Montreal, but which somehow seems closer.

I wish I could read Elisapie's mind to see how she imagines Kingsbury. How can a kid who has only known the tundra picture a tiny farming village deep in the Eastern Townships? Elisapie's summers have never been filled with the smell of cut hay and the tickle of long grass on bare legs. I would love to see what Kingsbury looks like in her head.

Elisapie straddles childhood and the world of adults. Sometimes she's still clearly a tiny little girl, and sometimes it seems she's already left for the troubled waters of her life as an adult. Like when I see her whiz by at the wheel of her mother's quad. Elisapie is thirteen years old now, that sensitive age when everything can suddenly change, go off the rails. Elisapie was adopted, like so many other children in this village. Adoption is so simple for you, though you're brilliant at complicating everything else. I love you so much for loving other people's children as your own, so simply. Anyway, children here really do belong to the whole village.

Just like in Africa. How bizarre… How can that be, that two different parts of the world, so far from each other, have so much in common?

Actually, it's not weird. Everybody everywhere in the world is basically the same. Except Western people. Indian time, African time, Mexican time, it's all the same time. We're the ones who live life all wrong, and yet we're so convinced of being right.

.

In your world, Eva, families who can support several children don't hesitate to take in those who weren't born in the right place. Sometimes it's great, but other times it ends badly.

Nathan terrorizes all the kids in Salluit. He knows who his mother is. He knows that she kept his big sister, but left him behind. Nathan lives with one of the most respected families in Salluit but he behaves like a real bully. Nathan makes me mad sometimes because he picks on the weakest kids, but when I see him desperately trying to see his mother, I forgive him.

Nathan-the-bully is dangerously intelligent. He might be prime minister some day. On the other hand, he might end up in prison. It's not only the under-twelve crowd who live in fear of him. Nathan has been aiming higher. He pointed a knife at old Suzanne, a woman in her late sixties who personifies strength. She is the polar version of Mother Theresa; she's the embodiment of Judeo-Christian devotion and self-sacrifice.

Suzanne has been a sixth-grade teacher here in Salluit for fifteen years. She is as tired as Lauren, but continues to hold down the fort, and never complains. "I'll do another year. I can still do it. The mortgage isn't paid yet." Suzanne became a widow way too young. She doesn't have the means to leave Salluit. Not yet. But it isn't true that she's here for the money. Not Suzanne.

Suzanne gets up at dawn every day to prepare her famous egg sandwiches, which she sells at the school all year round. She uses the money to send her best students on trips south. Nathan pointed his knife at *Suzanne*.

13

THE RCMP INVESTIGATORS must have been tearing their hair out, if they had any. Hair, I mean. I imagine them bald; I guess I watch too many movies. I'm sure they have grilled enough tough suspects over their career, but this might have been the first time they had to deal with an Inuk. This might have been the first time they found themselves with someone who doesn't talk, not because he's hiding something, but because he just doesn't talk. You Inuit, you really don't talk, whereas we white people talk too much. I so agree with you, Eva. If you knew how many incredibly boring conversations we have to put up with, day after day!

The investigators probably had no difficulty obtaining confessions. It's not like you to hide something you've done, even something really terrible. I beat my wife; I wrecked my boss's car; I spent my whole paycheque on alcohol. But I'm sure they'll never get any details about what happened, and they'll never find out why it happened. I won't either, Eva. I will never know why, and it's already killing me. Why did he do that, Eva? Why?

I can't ask anyone because nobody will want to answer me. This is your tragedy; I'm not supposed to put my big white nose in your business. You hate it when we don't mind our own business. But I wish I could just say, please just let me say: I loved her too. Please, please explain to me why I will never see her again.

14

They're really nice when they're sober.

Alcohol is like a full moon. Even the sweetest people turn into werewolves. Maybe that is why we're constantly vacillating between beauty and ugliness. By evening, if everything balances out, we've made it through another day. In the evening I go home and this woman, drunk out of her mind, shouts her lungs out at her four-year-old daughter. The little girl empties all the tears from her little body as her mother drags her toward God-knows-what private hell. What do you do when that happens? Do you grab the child and run home and hide her there? The picture of them begins to blur in my head. Now the mother is a little girl who is being shouted at by another mother who is also a little girl; they are Russian dolls, one within another, an infinite line of screaming, drunk mothers who turn into crying little girls, all the children, Russian dolls.

It's the children who fill my days and who stay on my mind long afterwards, in the evening, in the middle of the night, my dreams filled with children and Russian dolls. There are some who return more often. Jobie, for instance, is pretty much always there, like a piece of metal lodged in my chest. He's got the eyes of a caribou that has broken its foot. There was this young caribou in the tundra once, a baby lying there, all alone against the big rocks. It got up painfully when it saw us and that's when we saw it too: it ran away on three legs, the fourth one dangling behind it in this weird way. I wondered if it was going to suffer for very long and if it would die all alone, abandoned by the others who can't afford to keep the weak ones in their herd.

They say that your ancestors sometimes left old people behind. They were abandoned for being useless: infertile, unable to hunt, unable to give life and to feed it, life that is merciless in January's burning cold. They died alone, hoping the blizzard would finish them off quickly and that they wouldn't have to suffer for too long.

Today old people don't have to worry about that anymore. There are the heated, well-lit Kativik Municipal Housing Bureau dwellings. There is the Northern and the Co-op where you can find stuff to eat without having to wield a harpoon. But there are also dozens of Jobies with their injured caribou gaze. It was early in the morning. They found him on the road to the airport. Ten years old at the most, wearing a t-shirt, all curled up in a ball on a wooden board in front of a shack, fast asleep. The police brought him to the hospital. Sure, they'll take care of his hypothermia, but who will take care of the rest?

The North doesn't make room for those who can't fight.

The kids here are aware of it really young, and so they apply the law of the tundra, terrorize Evie because she's not normal. If she lived in the South they'd know exactly what's wrong with her, but up here Evie is the only one who gets herself, and who gets picked on by other kids. Luckily there's Louisa to keep her company, Louisa her big sister, an angel in the snow, beautiful and gentle Louisa. Louisa watches over Evie. Louisa, tiny protector to those who are even more vulnerable than herself.

Evie, Louisa, the others and I, gone to swim in the waterfalls. Shrieks of joy, the huge smiles of a gang of kids splashing around in the glacial water from the mountain. It's twelve degrees. I share their happiness but I will never take off my coat. Later, the little girls are amazed at how cold my hands are, and carefully warm them in their own, these children who are never cold and who are always afraid that my hands will freeze. I love the way they worry about me.

Evie walks so slowly that we will never get to the village. I grab her hand, firmly, and force her to walk at my pace. For a few long minutes I force her to abandon her own comfortable stroll until we at least come within view of some Salluit houses. Evie is exhausted. I feel bad, and drop her hand. Evie stops, of course, jabbers something I fail to understand, of course, and points to a big white rock behind us. But the rock is not a rock, it's a snowy owl, a magnificent snowy owl that soars, spreading its white sails, and in two flaps of its wings is far above our heads, huge in the northern sky.

Evie and I smile with the same joy; none of the others saw a thing.

15

BELOW THE KIDS are the dogs, the loyal allies of the Inuit for centuries, discarded since the arrival of snowmobiles. Sure, snowmobiles are faster, but try asking one to find your campsite by itself. These magnificent dogs, all mongrels, but magnificent mongrels: huskies, *ijangus,* Malamutes, German Shepherds, Labradors, Golden Retrievers, more and more mixed, like kids these days: white, black, Middle Eastern.

They are born at the end of June, just in time for my arrival. The mothers, whose stretched teats hang almost all the way to the ground, carefully hide their pups under houses and sheds. We can hear their little puppy noises here and there, a sharp, wet sound, the sound of life beginning, full of promise, like the Arctic summers. They grow fast; their sturdy puppy legs hint at future stature. They wander farther and farther away. Some follow me. I don't have enough hands to pet and hold them all. I dig my fingers and my face into their thick fur, jump back laughing at the coolness of a snout. Every single time I tell myself to protect my heart, for northern dogs will break it every single time. But can you really stop a heart from loving?

When I leave in the fall, I know I will never see them again. Some time during the fall, or in the winter at the latest, someone will give the signal. Too many stray dogs, too many dogs that don't belong to anybody, too many dogs running around in gangs that could become dangerous. If you want to keep your pet, bring it inside or keep it tied up on the night of the purge. On that night, those dogs that seem too free to belong to anyone will be slaughtered by people especially hired for that purpose. You'll come across frozen carcasses all over the place during the winter; they are the last relics of these splendid beasts who died too young, the way most Inuit do.

They'll break your heart along the way, these dogs. You will become attached to them, feed them, tame them, and then you'll find them dead on the side of the road. Alex lost two animal friends like that; he had secretly dreamed of training them for dog sledding someday. Alex can't stop his heart from loving; it will fall in the same trap again this year. I will have my heart stolen too, even if I haven't forgotten my favourite yet. He used to follow me from one end of the village to another, joyfully trotting along on his big fat legs, the legs that foretold his future size. He would let out happy whines when I pet him, and he never deprived himself of the pleasure of licking my face. I had gotten to the point where I daydreamed about having a husky in a two-bedroom apartment in the city. I would walk quietly on his street and feel thrilled whenever he suddenly appeared. The driver of the van didn't see him appear. He crashed into him. My favourite, lying on his side, softly whimpering. The driver stopped, got out, suffocated the dog. It only took a few seconds to finish him off. The driver pushed the carcass toward the ditch, got back in his van and kept going. Me looking at my favourite, not yet stiff at the side of the road. I hadn't found a name for him because I thought that would prevent me from getting attached. I just called him "my favourite."

And I hear them making fun of me, I hear them, the cynical ones, the fervent supporters of good old common sense, proclaiming there are lots of worse things in life than dying dogs. I hear them enumerate all the social problems that already exist in Nunavik. I hear them tell me all the problems that need to be solved first, as if each problem in life had its place on a long list of priorities. I hear them finding me ridiculous to cry over my favourite and all the other ones, like the beautiful Labrador mix that I had found a home for in the South. I hear them tell me that the dogs can wait, and I wonder when they will get around to the things on that list that they consider priorities.

During the 1950s, the federal government proceeded to slaughter the sled dogs on a massive scale in order to force the Inuit to settle down in one place. Fifty years later, they paid them millions in compensation. That's the way to do it: make a mess and then redeem yourself with piles of money. But thank God, they learned their lesson, these bloody nomads. Now they do it themselves, they slaughter their own dogs on a massive scale.

16

LAUREN MANAGED to survive Raglan Money Day. One more wrinkle, her heart a bit more worn out, but solid as a rock under the neon lights that light up the empty aisles of the Northern Store, despite all the sleep she missed. Once a year, Lauren and her husband go back to their native Manitoba for five weeks, but the rest of the time they work like maniacs. Almost all white people work like maniacs; maybe that's why they resent those Inuit who don't do anything. They are at the worksites from before seven in the morning until nighttime. They collapse with fatigue in the canteen, almost falling into their plates. Then they sink into the sofa, one millimetre at a time, in front of the TV before dragging their long male bodies to bed.

Up on the roofs they are redoing, they see me go by, flanked by my group of kids, as usual, going off to kayak or fish or pick blueberries. What they wouldn't give to join us.

They betray their envy by teasing me about my supposed idleness. And yet, I work. I am completely and faithfully devoted to my little polar-bear cubs. Every day I come up with a thousand and one activities to keep them occupied on these long summer days, because even the ones who claim to hate school get bored once it's over, and they have nowhere to go between the overcrowded home where they have to fight over the video game remote and the dusty roads they have walked around and around a hundred times. I work just as hard as the construction guys, but for them I might as well be on vacation: I'm lazy because I have Saturday and Sunday off. They think I should honour and revere them because they work seven days a week, because they are there to replenish their bank accounts and because they wouldn't even know what to do with a day off because, of course, there is nothing to do here. They come for a month or two or three or four or five, and they leave again without having learned a single word of Inuttitut, without having ever gone fishing, tasted caribou, without learning that to attract good weather you have to go up on the mountain and bare your bum, the Inuit version of the rosary on the clothesline. But there is no way I would understand: I only come here in the summer. I get the midnight sun and the mild July afternoons. I don't know anything about the months of murderous cold and darkness that kill as much as a blizzard can. I have it easy.

You have it so easy. You spend two months here, you walk around, you go boating, and then you go home. You don't know, but February here is fucking long. We all lose our minds. Everyone is crazy, but it's more obvious here. You can't hide your madness here. Everyone can see it. You can't have a secret garden. That stuff that only belongs to you, stupid stuff that you know is stupid but you do anyway. Well here, everyone knows about it. Everyone knows everything, all the time. And then in February, when there is fuck all to do here, that's all you've got, life plus everyone else's madness.

Yeah, Alex, I know.

Was it to survive February that you welcomed Alaku into your life? Because madness is easier to live through when there are two of you, or because hers is worse than yours? Was it to console yourself that you brought Alaku into your life? I was so mad at you, Alex, so mad that you actually preferred a twenty-year-old alcoholic junkie, a poor girl who hadn't finished high school and does nothing all day except drink and smoke. I was so mad.

Because I, of course, am the queen of England, because I am brilliant with a brilliant future, I'm the ideal woman coming straight from an ideal family, because I make great speeches about white arrogance and look how I'm just like them. I think I'm so much better than your poor Alaku, I can't imagine that faced with choosing between the two of us, you would choose her. I try to convince myself that she was a crutch you needed at the time, a temporary crutch, and I never asked you if you loved her.

Did you love her, Alex?

I was so mean, I made fun of you, I told everyone about your problems, and all my friends obviously confirmed my big-headed belief that I was the ideal woman. Of course, I was a hundred times better than her. You didn't know what you were doing, it wasn't going to last.

And it didn't last. Did you love her, Alex?

I know that she loved you, anyway. And that for months you were her hero, the one who helped her quit drinking and smoking, the one who patiently listened as she told the story of each of her traumas, the one who motivated her to go to work every day and to get there on time. The one who taught her tenderness and pleasure, who showed her that making love was wonderful, and not an unpleasant obligation you had to put up with while clenching your teeth and waiting for it to be over.

And I tell myself that I should find you wonderful to have been able to do all of that, but I can't manage it; I just keep wondering how you could find it so easy to make love with her when it was so difficult for you with me. Because in addition to finding myself a better woman, I find myself more beautiful, of course, because I am the queen of contempt, just look at me.

But it didn't really last, that grand role of knight in shining armour. One day the traumas were too much for your patience. They scared away the white saviour. The time you went to Kuujjuaq, that time when because you were going away for a few days, she wanted to force you to make love to her because otherwise, you were going to cheat on her. Everyone knows the story of your break-up because there is no room to hide the crazy parts of your life here. And I happily contributed to all the gossip, helping to pass on every little sordid detail: Alaku hitting you in the face, you having to defend yourself for a good two hours until the police arrived, the broken objects and the complete trashing of your apartment. It allowed me to be smug and crow about how right I'd been.

I'm so sorry.

And you were angry with yourself. You stayed with her until you couldn't take it anymore, you didn't want to abandon her. You knew that the break-up would destroy all the progress of the last few months and that from that point on, the alcohol, drugs and violence would return. And I kept kicking you while you were down—with glee—as the white knight turned into the bastard and you kicked her out of your oasis of an apartment to send her back to where she came from, to the chaos of an overcrowded home where she could be at the mercy of any drunk and disgusting uncle.

I'm so sorry.

It's so hard to be a hero, such a burden. Alaku, and we might as well say all the other young women in the village, all those who are waiting for their white knight, the one who won't cheat on them or beat them or drink like a fish, who will have a real job that will actually allow them to give their kids a decent life. Alex, handsome Prince Charming, your horse in the ditch and the princess knocked right off it, upside down with her legs in the air, forgive me. You have no idea of the awful things I said about you. You think I'm a good person, you can't even imagine that I would do something like that to you. You think I am too good for you, my lovely friend, forgive me. When pain slides over into bitterness, a heart can be seized by the strangest impulses.

And I still love you, and I always will, even if you have lost a few pieces of your own puzzle, even if you run away to the edge of the earth to escape from nice girls, especially the ones who love you, even if you are unhappy, whether alone or in a relationship. You are dragging around a wounded soul, even if you have never been raped, beaten or mistreated; you understand Alaku's torments as if you had grown up in the tundra and not in a quiet little town in the south of the province.

And I really want you to be happy, I swear, with whomever you want. I will still love you.

17

AANATUQ AND I SITTING on a rock. We follow the fjord with our eyes, all the way to the strait. Aanatuq shows me the way to Ivujivik, a long, full day by boat to get to the next village. Aanatuq has done it lots of times with his grandfather. I never had a grandfather, and if I had one, I doubt if he would have brought me seal hunting. Aanatuq didn't bring back a seal the last time. It was Sunday and apparently Jesus doesn't want us to hunt on Sunday. From our rock we can see Salluit's beautiful white church. It shines in the sun. Aanatuq chooses this moment to confide, "I used to smoke weed a long time ago."

A long time ago. What does that mean, exactly, when you're ten years old? Aanatuq is living his life backwards; he never lost his innocence because he never had any, but, arriving at the threshold of adolescence with the wisdom of an old man, he has decided to make peace with his demons. Aanatuq will never be Andrew or Saala, children whom I leave happy and free at the end of the summer only to find broken and lost the following year, without ever understanding what happens between the ages of ten and eleven in this village at the ends of the Earth.

Maybe it's the baggage they're carrying that is just too heavy, maybe it's the weight of all of these Shakespearean tragedies that stick, so early, to their little bodies. For Andrew, maybe it's his mother who killed herself before he started school, and for Saala maybe it's her alcoholic father. Maybe they manage not to think about it too much when they are younger, but later the reality finally gets to them, sinks in. Maybe.

18

AND YOU DIE. You never stop dying. There are all these stupid accidents that could be avoided, there is the merciless tundra that never gives you a chance, there are all these diseases that we don't have anymore, like tuberculosis, but which still attack you because of your mid-nineteenth century sanitary conditions. There is all that and, as if that weren't enough, on top of everything else, *you kill yourselves*, Christ!

If you weren't already dead, Noah, I would kill you. No, I would scream until you woke up: *What the hell were you thinking, what the hell were you thinking, what the hell were you—*

Don't you realize how loved you are, for fuck's sake, don't you see how you are loved even more than you love yourselves? But right now, Noah, I hate you, I swear I hate you, what the hell were you thinking, you asshole, you fucking idiot? *Fuck, fuck, fuck*, that's not how it's supposed to work. We aren't supposed to ask about a friend we haven't seen for a few months and find out that he's dead; we're not supposed to ask, "How's Noah doing?" and hear, "Oh, he died, you know; with the wisdom of his seventeen years he decided he had seen enough, so he shot a fucking bullet into his head. Because everyone has a gun, and everyone knows how to use one, thank you, good night."

And if you had just stopped to think for a moment, with your tiny idiot brain, you might have recalled that there are a whole bunch of people who love you. You could have thought twice before shooting yourself in the head, actually, you could have done about a million things instead of that, instead of shooting a stupid bullet into your tiny sparrow brain. What the hell were you thinking, you fucking idiot?

You're dead now, and you don't care, you don't give a shit about the rest of us who are still here and who will be missing you for the rest of our lives. I can't take it. It's too much. I can't keep leaving this place and each time wonder who will be next, who will be the one I won't see anymore, the one who won't be there next year when I come back. I can't take this.

19

So, do they sniff gasoline? Glue?

Honestly, people, get with the times! Gasoline and glue are so yesterday. Sure, there will always be a few who prefer vinyl, but today we have access to everything, even out here in caribou-eater country. Crack, pot, hash, amphetamines, cocaine: ask and you shall receive. A nice big glass of vodka will make it go down easier, Vodka Smirnoff at two hundred bucks for a ten-ouncer, a decent vintage. Everyone always wants to hear the sordid stuff, the scandalous, juicy, violent, troubling stuff. Every expatriate from the South has his horror story to tell. At parties with white people, I don't know if I am listening to compassion or morbid curiosity.

After a good hour of a particularly edifying monologue, Philippe the engineer asks me what I do, presuming that I am generously paid, like him. No, not really. Stupefaction: why am I here then?

Because I love it.

Poor Philippe. You can't believe your ears. Yup, Philippe, there are people who don't come up North just to make money. Personally, I love it here. I love the kids, the people, the language, the dogs, the landscape, the midnight sun, the aurora borealis, the caribou, the tundra, the mountains, the walks. I love it when there are ten of us in the back of a pickup going down the hill from the airport with the wind in our faces. I love the steamships lying majestically in the bay and all the surrounding comings and goings. I love the fjord, no matter its colour and its level of agitation. I love picking mussels at low tide and smiling inside as I tell myself that I have hunted my own supper. I love the belugas' white backs that burst through the surface of the water when I've been good. I love the kids returning from the marina with a fishing trophy almost bigger than themselves, the fabulous Arctic char. I love lying down on the rocks on mild days and staring out at the Hudson Strait, which calls to me, in a whisper. I love starting the engine of a quad by pulling the rope, because it looks more macho. I love the fact that everyone knows my name. I love the ground that shakes when a herd of caribou runs by. I love the village that pretends to be a ghost town when the fog lifts. I love picking blueberries and not bringing a single one back because I spent the whole time stuffing my face, sitting on my ass in the moss and lichen. I love it here.

•

There are three categories of white people who come up north: the adventurers, the missionaries and those who come for the money. Unfortunately, a fourth category exists too: the social misfits. Those who can't function in the South and who go into exile with the Inuit in order to blend in with the chaos here. They're generally men. They find themselves a wife, make a lot more children than they can feed and are quietly supported by various people in the village. Philippe, I'm pretty sure you're in the third category.

And what about you, which category are you in?

I don't know, I never know, I never fit into any category anywhere. An adventuring missionary, I guess, but I'm not a saint; I don't have the self-denial and humility of Mother Theresa. I am terribly proud, I like to succeed where others fail, I like taking a machete and opening a path, carrying out impossible missions and then saying, that was easy, what's next? Everyone is always congratulating me for my devotion to the children up here, but they forget how much I receive in return. They forget that if I don't move, I just wither away. They forget that there is a voice inside me screaming to leave wherever I am and go somewhere else. They forget that for me, a summer in the city is like being a plant without water, they forget that I fell in the magic potion and that I lose my balance when I have no menhir to carry. They forget that I yearn for so much, everywhere, all the time, that sometimes I can't sleep because I can't wait for tomorrow, or next week, or next month. Sometimes I crumble from exhaustion and then I promise to slow down, but it never lasts. I am in the whirlpool of an above-ground swimming pool; I spin around until I create a current that is almost destructive. And then, suddenly, when the waves spit me out on Salluit's shore, I feel strangely calm, and I take it easy for two months. Even if the Inuit also manage to wear me out.

Every time I go away I feel guilty. I feel bad for the people I leave, wherever I am, wherever I go, in both directions, from Montreal to the North, from the North to Montreal, from Montreal to all the places around the world where I have been roaming since I was old enough to buy a plane ticket. When I leave, I feel like staying. When I come back I feel like leaving. I carry the ones I love in my heart. But you're always alone at the airport.

I feel guilty about my rich country, my unbroken family, my education. I need to put out fires and save children, I need to do something in this rotten world, I need to run from one gang of helpless, abandoned people to another. I need to; otherwise, I might just sit and cry or hurl bombs at something. When it isn't the misery of the North, it's that of the South. The faces of Inuit children follow me to Haiti and then everything gets mixed up, Creole and Inuttitut, chocolate skin with almond eyes, the cold and the heat. Fuck Canada, fuck France, fuck the United States and Spain, all bastards, colonizers, slave-drivers. And I am dying; it's killing me, not being up to the task. I will never be able to sleep; the whole world is full of assholes who only think about filling their pockets. How can we possibly make up for all their shit?

While girls my age buy houses and make babies, I have other plans: I collect stories that don't go anywhere. There's a hole in my heart because I don't have a man who loves me and who would have children with me, but I have everything else. I yearn for everything, everywhere, all the time.

Actually, come to think of it, maybe I'm a social misfit.

20

I GO BY YOUR HOUSE almost every day. It's not your house anymore. Someone else, or probably, a bunch of people, grabbed it as soon as it became available. Probably a few lucky people were able to leave the shack where fifteen of them had been living all crammed together, to come and live at your house. They left the pretty lace curtains on the windows. There are these funny, random whims of vanity here in the North; sometimes, a little lace on a window and the house isn't the same as its neighbours, as all the houses on the street, as all the houses in the village, identical from one end to the other, from one village to the next. Houses built by civil servants, solid and utilitarian, with no time for style, no time to bother with creating different designs; if they had wanted to make art, they wouldn't have chosen the public service. There are four streets in Salluit and I pass by your house almost every day. Two men in front of your house are arguing. They pause as I jog by.

I love you! May I have your number? Can I run with you?

These guys are polite, almost romantic. Sometimes it's *I want to fuck with you*; *I love you* is less harsh. Northern men are like northern women; they also want to taste Southern whiteness, but they rarely get the opportunity: the construction camps here only hire white men. Sometimes they manage to, though; sometimes a teacher or a nurse will succumb to their crude seduction techniques. Sometimes they settle down past the tree limit and they, too, make children; she who takes a husband takes a country. Sometimes they find themselves the protagonists in stories as sad as your own. Jane came here from Nova Scotia. First, she succumbed to the charm of one guy, who gave her a daughter, and then, five years later, a different guy, who gave her a son. Jane works at the Co-op. She lives in a bedroom at the hotel with two kids from two different fathers. This place is starting to lose its charm. Jane is thinking of going back to Cape Breton.

Sometimes, too, white women are just looking for a little short-term exoticism, something to warm up the long winter nights, something to satisfy their fantasies of cold-taming hunters—and they break some warrior hearts. Arianne set her heart on Johnny. Johnny was barely nineteen years old. Like a northern version of Dalida, Arianne had tons of fun. She learned to hunt and to tear her catches apart, limb for limb, all by herself. Arianne tore Johnny's heart apart before returning South to start a life with a serious boy who had a promising future.

21
Low tide on the Foucaud River. A field of rocks stretches from the fjord to the bottom of the tundra, between two cliffs framing the magnificent river. Blond sand licks the riverbed's muddy bottom, dried up for now. The sun turns the fjord into a golden ocean. Shines so brilliantly it makes your eyes burn. There are some days, like those rainy, five-degrees-in-July days, when I just want to get out of here. But there are others that make me want to settle here in the tundra, between the blinding fjord and the river that splits the rock with quiet assurance, days of sunshine and low tide on the Foucaud River.

There are mild days like the kindness you find in the people here; sweet, like Charlie, who picks me up in his truck and drives me to the water pump to fill the water jugs for the guys from Kewatin, who've stopped here for fresh supplies before going back to sea. Charlie battled fire a few years ago, when flames took the village by surprise as it was sleeping, ravaging the Co-op building in a few hours. Charlie, like many others, ran toward the blaze and didn't stop for a single second until the fire was under control. Charlie is always ready to lend a hand. He never asks questions and he never asks for anything in return. He's ready to put out fires and give lifts to girls he finds lugging around giant water jugs on foot.

There are days of tenderness, days when kids wave to you, days when grandfathers stop their quads to give you a lift, days when I would run into you, Eva, your eyes sparkling and your smile radiant, beautiful like the *Maria Desgagné* moored in Salluit Bay, days when we would chat in front of your house with the lace curtains. Sometimes you'd had a bit to drink, but it was all right, alcohol sort of suited you, gave you those shining eyes, made you talk a bit faster. You weren't the only one to drink in your village, which is supposedly dry: there's no place to sell it, and only limited access to ordering it, a maximum of seventy-five dollars' worth a month per person, prohibited to those whose names appeared on the list. The blacklist, the fateful list, the list of people and transgressions committed under the influence of alcohol: disturbing the peace, vandalism, domestic violence, suicidal behavior, impaired driving. Pages and pages of offences, for a village of thirteen hundred inhabitants. Pages and pages of people who resort to contraband.

They pay more, but they get what they want. And they always want the same thing: ten-ouncers of Smirnoff vodka. The whole village is littered with the empty plastic bottles. Any idiot can see that more than seventy-five bucks of booze per person gets drunk here.

Another offence that could go on that blacklist: having kids and never taking care of them, because kids conceived under the influence of alcohol don't count. That's what they tell me. Oh, Jobie, are you a kid who doesn't count? A lot of people hide behind this oh-so-practical rule. Like Willy, the Sun King of Salluit. The most handsome man for kilometres, husband and father to three legitimate children. Willy has tons of kids who don't count. Willy got married last fall, elegant in his smoking jacket, proud and respectable before all the well-wishers who filled the church, and his three kids, the ones who count.

22

SO TELL ME, what was so great about your Jimmy? What did he have that the others didn't? Was it that he made you forget that school principal of yours? Made you forget another white guy gone without ever contacting you again, gone without a care, without ever thinking how much you would miss him, gone to continue leading his life, the life he'd had before the blip in it, as if you were just a blip, a digression, not anyone important in his personal story. That has got to be painful, after a while. If it can make you feel any better, you were not the only one. But no, that won't make you feel better, I know. You weren't the only one. The North is full of heartbroken girls, girls who love guys so much, guys who took them for soapstone carvings: a cute souvenir that brings back happy times, but nothing else, once back home in the South.

There's Molly, the girl from the hotel: three happy years with Simon, her policeman, three happy years gone without a warning last winter, when Simon went on his vacation. Down South for his usual two weeks off, he managed to get a job in his hometown and never set foot back in Salluit. He had his things sent to him by plane. Molly would have liked to say goodbye. Molly's eyes are wild with pain.

Was it because of these blips, these digressions, that you threw yourself at Jimmy's neck? What was so special about him that you accepted being his number two, beautiful, funny, kind, intelligent you, who deserved to be in first place. What was so special about him?

It was your beauty that killed you, Eva. We knew it would happen someday, ever since the day you dared to walk around in a skirt in the village, ever since that day when everyone in Salluit saw your gorgeous legs, and a crazy woman threw herself on you at the Co-op in a fury because your beauty had thrown off its polar coverings and revealed itself to the whole world. You defended yourself okay, but that black eye did darken your face for a little while.

It's dangerous for beautiful women here. You could get pregnant, or raped. Or someone else's boyfriend could find you pretty. Because everything is always the woman's fault. Girls who get cheated on rarely get mad at their partners, or at least never as much as they do at their rivals. The graffiti that springs up everywhere does not lie: *fucking bitch*, *slut*, the mark of the outraged female, the signature of women who will stand by their men, and who will avenge their pain on the women who dared lay hands on their boyfriends—the whores, the witches, the devil herself, nothing less.

But I can't let them do that to you, Eva. I can't let them drag your name in the mud, spit on your beauty. I refuse to condemn you for having loved someone else's husband. I can't let them crush someone because she is too beautiful, too luminous, too threatening to everyone else. I can't let them stop the stars from shining. I won't let them slow down all the comets because they make people jealous. I cannot tolerate this idea that some people have, that you got what you deserved. I want to carry you like a flag in the streets of Salluit, wave you around. I want to throw you in the faces of all those good people and scream at them that they are wrong. Eva, I want you to come back.

23

GINA ENTERED YOUR CLASSROOM, her face swollen. You clench and unclench your fists.

It happened in Kangiqsujuaq, following a volleyball tournament. Apparently, she looked at another guy. He didn't like that. She was on the ground. He was beating her, kicking and punching her. There were about twenty people there. And they just watched.

Alex gulps down some wine. It takes a lot of wine to forget that a fifteen-year-old child can get beaten up by her sweetheart without anyone batting an eye. A lot of wine to hear that she should have just not looked at another guy. Gina's dad hits Gina's mom and nobody bats an eye there either. Gina's mother didn't tell Gina to break up with her boyfriend.

You don't know how you managed to teach math class that day, to Gina, sitting in one corner, her eye crimson, and to Jusua, her violent boyfriend, in the other. You were afraid of losing it, of beating Jusua with kicks and punches until he was as puffy and swollen as Gina.

We finish the bottle. We don't talk about Alaku, but I know you're thinking of her. Alaku, Gina, all the ones you can't save. You say this will be your last year. The North is rough on the heart. The North is a child, shunted around from one foster family to another, who doesn't want to be rejected again. It will make your life impossible until your heart can't take it anymore, so you leave before you explode. And then it can say: *You see, you're leaving me.* Because you're always being abandoned. We just keep turning you into these blips, these digressions, brief adventures that we want to experience for a while before going back to our tidy lives in the South, or going somewhere new, somewhere which now seems much more attractive than your northern exoticism.

I'll abandon you too, Eva. One day I will leave your body rotting at the bottom of the fjord. I will stop desperately searching for you under the ripples. I won't leave any children with blue, almond eyes scattered around your village, and I won't have broken any warrior hearts, but I will abandon you, all of you.

I wish I could say that I am better than the others, but I'm not. I can't promise that I'll stay. Every time the summer ends I wish I could swear to come back the following year but I can't. I am as flighty as a starlet.

24

Jess. You know the first time I saw you, I didn't find you pretty? I hadn't understood your face. And then one day the pieces came together: your big green Métis eyes, your milky skin, your huge smile, your long dark hair, plus the slenderness – you got that from your Métis heritage too. You're beautiful.

You're my little Inuit sister, Jess. I know, I'm not your mother, and maybe I should love you a little less. Your knuckles black and blue from hitting the wall, loud knocks in these houses that are too used to being struck. You're a little flower atop a pile of steaming manure, an orchid in a garbage dump, a daisy in a January blizzard. Your last name is Lapointe—so exotic among the Saviadjuks—in honour of the father you see once a year. The rest of the time it's just your mother, your mother and her bottle of booze, your shrieking mother. And maybe you will become a Russian doll one day too. Your little sister and your little brother are already fucked up. Don't worry, you took as good care of them as you could. I know.

One day your mother, completely pissed, crashed the school-board truck, and you ended up with broken knuckles. But it won't be long now. At the end of the summer, you'll leave for Kangiqsujuak, finish high school, and that may finally lead to college, far away from here. At college, you young things, students like you and your friend Aida, are so beautiful and intelligent. We all wish you the best. We have so much hope for every teenager who manages to finish high school, freed from the pain, misery and despair of your environment. Somehow, out of about fifty little chicks blessedly peeping away in kindergarten classrooms, fewer than ten graduate from high school. We are all here with so much hope for you, wanting, more than you, *praying* that you survive the shock that awaits you in Montreal, where alcohol is available everywhere, where, at night in your room at your college residence, you will lie in bed missing your dysfunctional families. Much too often, it doesn't work: they send you back to where you came from because you failed your tests, and you accept this defeat without thinking of trying again. And we are so much more disappointed than you are. Then we go back to dreaming. We pin our hopes on the next student who might end up making it.

We dream for Ryan, fifteen years old, a seed planted all crooked, a rare flower trying to make his way out of the darkness toward the sun in a flowerbed overgrown with poison ivy. At Ryan's house, it always smells like pot, twenty-four hours a day. Ryan's three little brothers aren't even five years old yet; they play half-naked in the street in front of the house. It smells like misery twenty-four hours a day at Ryan's house. Ryan dreams of going to live with a foster family, but nobody will take him, not him and not his three little brothers: his parents threaten anyone who would dare steal their children away from them. We dream for Ryan, the local hip-hop star, brilliant and talented. My God, let him survive to the age of eighteen, when he can finally escape. We have so much hope for you.

We hope so much and sometimes it works. Sometimes I get on the plane and am greeted by the ravishing Alacie, the pearl of Salluit. Four years of patient and monotonous work as a Northern Store cashier before becoming a flight attendant for Air Inuit. She is only the second Inuk to get a job with the company. I am so proud and happy for my sweet Alacie that my heart wants to burst from its rib cage to go cuddle with hers. My Alacie, flight attendant, neurosurgeon or Nobel Laureate in Chemistry, it's the same thing for me.

25

A MESS. Salluit is a teenager's bedroom. The high school's broken windows. The elementary school playground, next to the administrative centre.

Fuck you. Fucking school. Boring. I love you. I hate you. Bitch. Aida 2010. Jimmy + Mary. I love Tayara. Fuck you Jimmy. Salluit sucks. I hate school.

The kids jump with their feet together on the construction materials piling up here and there on street corners, stuff to repair what is broken before it breaks again, to build new stuff to better destroy it the next time. Bicycles, toys, mutilated and abandoned in the ditches. Plastic bags floating around. Thousands of empty Smirnoff bottles, Cadbury wrappers.

The swimming pool is still intact. It survived its first year, nailing shut the mouths of the cynics who are always ready to bet on how long the infrastructures will last, to protest against the waste of our precious tax dollars.

The graffiti will be painted over and the windows will be repaired, and that will last a couple of days or months; we'll see.

26

MID-AUGUST. Night has quietly returned. For a few weeks now, it has been stretching a little bit longer, just a few minutes each day, as the temperature also creeps down a tiny bit at a time. Your summers are so short; they go by so fast. The northern lights also make their timid return. The late summer lights hesitate as they appear, gentle and gradual as they spread their white halo, almost apologizing for their existence and for this announcement of the cold's return. They are nothing like the ones in the winter, those beauty queens that shatter the sky from one side to the other with their spectacular green rays.

Sitting in the moss, passing the bottle back and forth, the sweet almond taste of Amaretto still on the two pairs of lips melting against each other. It's cold, although above us the white beauties light up the sky. Down here, our bodies are warming each other up. I am like the Inuit; I found my prey around the camps—or maybe I'm the prey, spotted from the roofs the men fix. I don't know who tracked whom anymore.

If I sleep with one of the construction guys, maybe I will save a child. If I offer my body, maybe a little girl won't have to offer hers. There are the wise ones who take the initiative themselves, and those who are pimped out by an uncle or a father, in the shack behind the house. It's about as easy to miss as a polar bear in an igloo, but no one has ever seen or heard anything, of course not. There are respectable men, married men, family men, who don't care about other people's families, who fuck other people's kids without having to go to Thailand because the Inuit also have almond eyes; you must get the same feeling. And when you pay, you are allowed to do anything. The customer is always right. The customer can do what he wants and stick whatever he wants wherever he wants, even in the body of a twelve-year-old child.

There is this little girl with red eyes. She really likes marijuana. She is thirteen and can't afford to buy any, so it's a blowjob for a joint. It's the law of supply and demand. There's Julia, whose eyes have lost their light. Julia. Rumour has it, last winter, there were four of them from the construction site, four guys taking turns on your body, the body of a little girl. There are those that are paid and those that aren't, those that are asked for permission, those that are forced. There's Alaku and all her friends for whom it's normal to be raped all the time. There is sex, money and impunity, *Tunngasugit Salluni.*

There's the other Aida. Nineteen years old and too tired to work. Nineteen years old and never up before noon because of all the booze the night before. Oh, Aida. I give her shit when she lets me down; I say, "Jesus Christ, are you ever going to fucking make something of yourself, do something with your intelligence, for fuck's sake?" Aida was raped too, at the beginning of the summer. I didn't know. I'm sorry. And she was abused years earlier by her own father. Me, the clod, I give her a hard time for leaving a job. You know, sometimes I get pissed off because I can never get pissed off at anybody; there is always some huge drama in your lives which more than excuses every little lapse.

27

PINGUALUIT, AN INUIT WORD that means "pimple". You Inuit, you really have a way of naming things. So after the villages "Stench of Rotten Meat" and "Intestinal Worm," there is the National Park of the Pimple.

Tell me Eva, have you ever seen this marvel? A meteorite that came and crashed onto Earth more than a million years ago, a hole three and a half kilometres wide, four hundred metres deep, full of perfectly clear water, a lake that is now ranked third in the world for the purity of its water. Ever seen this marvel, Eva? Probably not. Most Sallumiut have never seen this beauty, except in photographs, even if it is located just thirty or so kilometres from your area.

At the foot of the crater, rich Swiss people unhurriedly sip their cups of tea. Nunavik: "our territory."

So two summers ago this rich American, this ninety-five-year-old fucker, comes here. He treats himself to a fly-fishing trip in Kangiqsualujjuaq. Ninety-five years old, filthy rich, but he didn't want to pay for insurance, the old fart. So, of course, he managed to dislodge his artificial hip while fishing. They had to go get him by helicopter, and when he got to Kuujjuaq, he refused to have an injection; he said our Third-World hospital was unsanitary. He was ready to pay fifty thousand dollars to have a Challenger bring him home. In the end, we convinced him to let us treat him. And afterwards, he went back in the helicopter to finish his fishing trip in Kangiqsualujjuaq.

The nurses laugh and take big sips of their liquor. They hate it when American tourists doubt their skills. They perform miracles every day, and these rich old assholes can just go fuck themselves.

28

A PRIME MINISTER visiting a village in the Canadian Arctic, all smiles, poses in the tundra. The tundra is good for some pretty gorgeous pictures, it's so damn photogenic. The Inuit are photogenic as well. The old people with their toothless smiles, the impish children, the women carrying babies in their hoods. On film, they look good enough to eat, magnificently wrapped in these splendid coats that they make themselves, their gazes at once piercing like those of hunters, and dreamy like poets. A prime minister wants to show the whole world the beauty of the Canadian Arctic.

Summer is renovation season. Denis the mechanic has a family of ten staying in his shack until the work on their house is finished. Denis and I stand in front of his shack and ask ourselves if that is the beauty of the Canadian Arctic, that or the melting glaciers. They make such gorgeous pictures, those melting glaciers.

Fall is eviction season. Your house doesn't belong to you, and when it's been too long since you last paid your rent, the

Municipal Office sends its bailiffs to kick you out. Oh, they're pretty nice at the Municipal Office. They wait until your debt is really huge, something like tens of thousands of dollars; at five hundred dollars a month, it would have to be ages since you last paid your rent. The bailiffs are nice too. They propose a deal before they take your sofas; they are ready to accept as little as ten dollars a month if necessary, but when the tenants refuse, they have to proceed, and suddenly there are ten people in the street, ten people who go invade the overcrowded house of a cousin, or settle for a shack, Denis's or someone else's. Last fall they evicted Tommy, a cancer patient who had never paid rent in his life. They came over while he was receiving treatments in Montreal and sawed his shack in half. The whole village was outraged, demanding an end to this, calling it *slavery*, nothing less. But the revolution never happened; it hasn't happened yet, and the Municipal Housing Office is still crumbling under its debts, struggling as usual to collect payments.

You know, Eva, I always do my best to defend you to everyone, but when a single mother works like a madwoman for miserable pay to make her rent, she doesn't understand why you get housing for free, paid for by her taxes, and this conversation ends, almost invariably, with: *So let them go back to their igloos if they're unhappy!*

Of course you won't go back to living in igloos, but sometimes I wonder if all this free stuff was such a good idea. Sometimes I think of Félix Leclerc; sometimes I say to myself, *Jesus Christ what an unholy mess* and I wish someone somewhere would tell me what the right answer is.

29

ULLURIAQ. "STAR". I'm not giving you a pretty nickname here. That's the actual meaning of your first name. Your star is definitely a good one. I don't know where you come from; I guess another miserable hole, for sure, but Lizzie had you stay with her, same as she did with Akisuk and Nathan, and as I'm sure she did with other children. I don't know how long you've lived with Lizzie, maybe since always. Maybe you never actually knew your own unhappy story. Maybe that's why you are so radiant.

You followed me like a duckling in the tundra, you and two little boys even tinier than yourself. You completely messed up my plan for this walk, which was supposed to be solitary and contemplative. Instead, you infused it with your own awkward poetry, and I turned into a wild goose thrilled to be teaching you to fly. We walked in the late afternoon sun, not saying a word, just smiling, needing no explanations in order to understand each other. Ever since that day, I've watched for your sweet little face every morning. You are happiness itself, happiness on two little legs. The only way you know how to be is joyful.

30

NO BODY, NO CEREMONY. They haven't found your body so I still hope for your return. I see you walking on the fjord like Jesus alighting on the North Pole. That would really please Lizzie, as well as all the others who go to the beautiful white church in Salluit every Sunday morning to absolve their sins. Because everyone can drink, fight, smoke, curse, fuck, abuse, lie, steal, destroy, rape, cheat, and come out as clean and white as a willow ptarmigan in January each Sunday after church; everyone starts over again until the following Sunday. The only unpardonable sin is abortion. Sometimes a girl will get in a quad and speed around the mountain, aim for holes and cracks in the snow on purpose, and if she's lucky, manage to dislodge her baby.

No body, no ceremony. They haven't found your body so I still hope for your return. You believe in all kinds of things here, so why can't I believe in your return? You believe in God and in Jesus, you believe in everything the missionaries shoved down your throat. I feel like shaking you, shouting that if God existed, he would do something for you, fuck! You believe in the Yeti; apparently he was seen in Puvirnituq last winter. You believe in evil spirits that can get you lost in the tundra.

Skidoonguaq. A phantom Ski-Doo. It sometimes appears in the tundra, far from the village. You think it's a real snowmobile, and the driver signals to you to follow him. But he loses you in a snowy desert. You never find the trail again. You're lost and you might freeze to death. You have to be super careful.

The phantom Ski-Doo makes me laugh way more than Jesus does, but I hold it in, careful not to offend sweet Sarah. Sarah stopped drinking more than ten years ago, when the polar bear gave her her chance.

I'd been arguing with my boyfriend. I'd been drinking. I went for a walk right to the edge of the village to have a good cry by myself. It was foggy, and I couldn't see more than two feet ahead. I went home an hour later; I was cold. I found out the next day that there had been a bear alert that night, in exactly the same place where I'd been.

The polar bear spared Sarah and she got her shit together. I am still waiting for your return, but animals are so much kinder than human beings.

31

NEWS TRAVELS FAST from one village to another because, of course, everyone has a cousin who lives somewhere, everyone flies the milk run, everyone has to take off, land, take off, land before arriving at their destination; broken telephone is still the best means of communication out at the ends of the world. News from Akulivik, a place no one's heard of, a place that people only ever hear about when something awful happens: some guy killed another guy yesterday. Just out of the tundra, still drunk on alcohol, sex and Northern Lights, Joanessie builds a fire on the rocky shore to sober me up. He's got a cousin in Akulivik, of course. A man found out that another guy had abused his daughter, so he made things right again with a bullet between the eyes. Welcome to the Far North. No one says please or thank you here; no one says they're sorry either. When you've done something wrong, you do something to make up for it, and if that's not possible, there's always a .22 gauge that will take care of it.

I don't have a .22 gauge, but sometimes I'm scared of what I would do if I had one. I'm afraid of snapping, of going postal in the construction camps and shooting all of those bastards who get off inside thirteen-year-old girls. I'm afraid of castrating them, one at a time, all of these pieces of garbage who spilled themselves on Julia. I can't stand it anymore, how all of these pigs get away without a scratch. And they'll tell me that that isn't how things go, that justice will be done, but justice doesn't do its job here; that's why so many people settle their scores by themselves.

Akulivik, yet another place that people only ever talk about when something awful happens. The last time I was there, the plane had trouble landing: the caribou had invaded the landing strip. Long minutes of circling the strip to scare away the animals and convince them to go back over the fence. When we took off, we flew over the herd that was running along the river like the stars of a photo shoot in *National Geographic*.

A shooting in Akulivik.

I'd really rather talk about the caribou.

32

INSTRUCTIONS FOR A YOUNG FOOL on his first trip north: watch where you put your penis. Up here, in the great Inuit lottery, you've got a good chance of drawing an unlucky number, and of getting way more than you bargained for. If you think that jealousy is cute, find it flattering to your male ego, it's because nobody has ever come over with a .12 gauge to accuse you of sleeping with his ex. Yup, young fool, everyone here has a weapon and knows how to use it. It's like in the Far West, just a bit colder. If you believe that jealousy is cute and find it flattering to your male ego, it's because nobody has ever banged on your door, wailing the whole time, all night, begging you to let her come in. If you believe that jealousy is cute and find it flattering to your ego, you stupid jerk, it's because nobody has ever asked you to throw your mistress into the fjord. Oh, Eva.

The young fool looks at me, uncomfortable, wondering why I've burst into tears.

Hey, don't worry. I'll be careful, I promise. I'll make sure I don't get shot. Don't cry.

I leave the young fool standing there and run towards Jimmy's house. Jimmy isn't home. He's rotting away somewhere in a prison cell in St. Jerome, but his wife is there. She'll never go to prison. Her hands are clean, but her heart is rotten. She's the one who uttered your death sentence, but she'll never be sentenced to anything herself.

She ate your heart raw, swallowed it down in one gulp. She got revenge on both of you, you at the bottom of the fjord, him buried deep in some prison. She is as free as air as you sink deeper and deeper into the sludge. I would dig you out with my bare hands. I wonder if it hurt a lot when he hit you. I am standing in front of Jimmy's house and his kids are playing in the sand. *You miss to me.*

33

THE END OF AUGUST. Time to go home. The green of the tundra is turning russet, sign that fall is on its way, and not far behind it, the long, cold darkness of winter. The North does this on purpose. As I get ready to leave, it will give me an absolutely gorgeous day, as if to taunt me and convince me to stay. No fog, not even a cloud, no chance that my plane will be grounded; no, today will definitely be the day that I take off. Bright sunshine, which transforms everything it touches into gold. Seen from above, everything is even more stunning. The fjord turns turquoise, the seabed displays its strange patterns, the cliffs shine like new shoes. The beauty is overwhelming and I feel like crying, of course.

Everyone gets off in Puvirnituq, the plane refuels, and me too. I frantically search for Andrew all over the airport. Andrew is my favourite human being in Puvirnituq, maybe in all of Nunavik and maybe even in the whole world. Andrew, my heart, my angel, my little bear, I am trying to find his round face, his wide smile, those bright eyes that he hides behind tinted glasses. Nineteen years old and way too mature. You people are often described as large children, yet you have some children who are like wise old men. Andrew, my heart, my angel, my little bear; Andrew smiles at me as if he were driving a race car rather than an airport maintenance cart. Andrew is always working, with Air Inuit for very little pay, and the rest of the time with the village kids, for nothing at all. One day, I asked Andrew why he refused to be paid.

This is my community. A few years ago, things went wrong, horribly wrong, out of control. I have to do something for my community.

Andrew doesn't want to give me any details, but behind those tinted lenses, you can see all the sadness of the whole world, as well as this heartbreaking will of his to keep me at arm's length from this madness. Oh, Andrew, if you only knew.

Andrew, my favourite human being in Puvirnituq, and maybe even in Nunavik, and maybe in the whole world, twenty minutes with Andrew to propel me farther away than all the gas in our plane's tank ever could.

In Inukjuak I look away from the plane window for a moment and my eyes settle on two young passengers boarding. In handcuffs. A lovely free trip to Montreal, a trip they may have made before and will probably make again, the usual courtroom to prison deal, including a free stay of a few months or a few years, an all-inclusive package deal popular with northern youth.

Inukjuak has come a long way, has come all the way from 1999, that awful year that witnessed its youth population decimated by nineteen suicides in one year. Nineteen suicides in one year is huge, but in a community of sixteen hundred people, the pain becomes horribly personal.

Inukjuak has come a long way, thanks to the women of the village who decided that this had to end; it was high fucking time. It was high fucking time they stopped piling up coffins on frozen ground while waiting for spring to return. It was high fucking time they stopped inscribing wooden crosses with dates of birth and death whose difference amounted to less than twenty years.

Inukjuak has come a long way from 1953. It has come back from being forced into exile by the Canadian government: half the village deported two thousand kilometres north, near Grise Fjord and Resolute in the High Arctic. Inukjuaq has come back from the time when the government wanted to ensure its Canadian presence up to its territorial limits because, in any case, they already survive really well in the cold, a little colder or a little less cold couldn't make much of a difference, right? They ended up coming back, finding their way home, but their history made less of a splash than *The Incredible Journey*; I'm still waiting for the movie.

Inukjuak has come a long way thanks to the village women who forced the men to wake up, rounded up the community, helped it pull itself together and heal, set up initiatives to fight against all this suffering. Inukjuak is shaky like a convalescent too long bedridden but standing resolutely now for its first steps into the sunlight.

.

Umiujaq is the next village. More displaced people. They came from Kuujjuarapik when the James Bay dam was built. We don't want to hear that all this comfort had a price, that modern Quebec and its lovely green energy, "Maîtres chez nous," is also "Maîtres chez eux;" but who would spare a thought for a few hundred Inuit from the cozy warmth of a Drummondville living room?

Finally, Radisson. Leaving the airplane, the scent of trees startles me after months of its absence, months without the smell of your trees. The tight rows of pines exhale a powerful perfume a few kilometres from the runway, as if to console me for the tundra I've just lost. As usual, there is a long wait in the airport, and I strum my guitar to pass the time. One of the young prisoners comes up to me to make a few special requests. I offer to let her play. I hadn't thought of the handcuffs, and the police officer isn't likely to give us permission. She has to make do with an old Shawn Phillips song and my smile, which is meant to tell her that she will come a long way too, one day.

34

MONTREAL. IT'S ALWAYS THE SAME. From the air the city seems to spread out endlessly, with its houses, skyscrapers, boulevards, lampposts, highways, McDonalds', shopping centres, parking lots. How many times could I fit Salluit into this desert of civilization? A hundred times? A thousand? Barely a hundred houses, two schools, a police station, two stores, a hotel, an arena, a daycare, City Hall, the church, the administrative centre, the community centre, the youth centre, the medical clinic, the municipal garage, the water reservoir, the pool, the port. How many times?

It's always the same. For a few days I will be like a foreign correspondent stuck in a war-torn country; there's always a few seconds' delay with the impeccably dressed news anchor in her comfortable Montreal studio. I will wander like a sleepwalker through the aisles of our gigantic supermarkets, stunned by the obscene abundance and by all of these products that will be thrown out when they are in better shape than anything you find in the North. I will ceaselessly search for a familiar face in every public place and end up feeling lonely, never running into a single smile, never hearing my name called out, its syllables resonating with joy. And one fine day, maybe at the exit of a metro station, downtown, probably, I will see some faces with almond eyes, a colourful *nasaq* on their heads like the last vestiges of Northern kingdoms, a wrinkled hand held out, some words pronounced in that rough English that is so familiar to me. Old, fallen warriors lost in the big city.

People wonder why you leave your territory to land on the merciless concrete of a city where you know no one, but it's simple. Basically it *is* to know no one; it's precisely that. In a village of four hundred people, it's hard not to see someone. When this someone has raped you or killed a member of your family, the Montreal metro can seem like a great place to be.

Maybe one day Jimmy will get out of prison and make his way from St. Jerome to Salluit. Maybe one day he will run into Elijah, your son, and maybe Elijah will find that the village is not big enough for both of them. If I ever see Elijah panhandling at the doors of the Atwater metro station, Eva, I promise I'll bring him home.

PART II

ELIJAH

1

SOME SAID SHE WASN'T YOURS. We'll never know if they were right. That's how it usually goes around here. In any case, they belong to the whole village. The children, I mean.

Many of you used to dream about pretty Maata; many wanted to taste her soft skin, her graceful neck, with the ends of her black hair delicately grazing its nape. Maata, barely sixteen, teasing you, setting you aflame with her little fairy fingertips. Maata never revealed the names of the men who had known her body, but the village whispers carried the news from one house to the other, powerful as the autumn winds. The whole village was talking about you, because you can't make a secret garden for yourself here. You can't dig a hole in the frozen ground and hide your great love, bury your warrior heart there, silently, at Maata's feet.

The village talked about Lucassie too: did he love her as much as you did? Lucassie and Elijah, two men for one woman, two men who had both pressed their lips in the hollow of her shoulder, only a few nights apart, two men who could have planted Cecilia in Maata's womb. And the whole village whispers: Which one? Which one? Which one? Both of you watched her belly grow, watched it grow with the rest of the village; both of you uncertain, neither knowing which of you would soon have a daughter, which one of you would be forever connected to Maata, which one?

She arrived one fall evening, your fall, which looks so much like our winter. You kept your worry to yourself, your fear that Cecilia would not make her way without breaking her delicate mother, but you worried for nothing, for Maata is even stronger than she is tiny. She arrived one fall night, without making a fuss, a lovely, calm baby, and Maata said that she was yours. You were only eighteen years old but you were a daddy now. Lucassie didn't say anything, accepting this defeat the way you do here most of the time: silently. Lucassie didn't want to fight, but the village continued to whisper behind his back, and behind yours.

You were happy anyway, happy standing next to Maata, baby in the hood of her parka, happy to feel your daughter's little fingers on your index, wrinkled with cold, happy to be a father, you, who had never known your own.

You kept the baby. You didn't give it to an aunt or to a cousin, as so many teenagers do, leaving your kids with someone or other without anyone worrying about it; the children belong to the whole village. Maata worked long hours at the Co-op, the baby carriage parked next to the cash. Sweet Cecilia never bothered her mother, or the customers. We white people are always telling you how to raise your kids, and we decide whether or not you are qualified to take care of them, but we don't tolerate ours in many places.

·

Your friend Aleisha didn't keep her baby. Aleisha, little queen of Salluit, the temperamental empress, the jealous diva, pushy and strident like wind in a crack in a wall. Aleisha the first lady of Salluit; she engraved her name in the skin of Tayara Nassak, the local hip-hop superstar. He belongs to her, and you had better not forget that, young ladies, and now she has him, by the balls and by the umbilical cord. Aleisha wanted her baby to be a heavy chain around Tayara's neck, but a baby is annoying and it cries all the time, so the baby went to live with a cousin in Ivujivik. But Tayara will never escape Aleisha; she calls him day and night and watches him from her window, and whenever she has the slightest suspicion, she rushes to his house and looks for the ghosts of girls under his bed. Tayara can't take it anymore, nor can his family. Aida, the little sister, now sleeps anywhere but at home.

"She enters the house smiling, says hello to my parents, asks me how it's going, gives my sister a piece of candy, pets the dog. Then she goes into his room and closes the door. And she roars."

For hours, Aleisha attacks Tayara with screams and accusations. It is like a knife attack that goes on for hours. She is mad at him for what he does, for what he doesn't do, for what she thinks he does. There are hundreds of you who have thousands of reasons to scream and shout, who suffer in silence, but Aleisha, who has never wanted for anything, screams all the time. And her noise manages to bury that deafening silence of yours.

There are some women who scream, and some men who let them: Tayara says nothing. He waits for the storm to be over, but she never calms down. Never. Tayara fell for her sweet ass and her sulky pout. He didn't know that those full lips would open on strong teeth that could shred him in a fury. He didn't know that Aleisha was one of those women who play Greek tragedies in a loop, Greek tragedies in which they have the lead role. He believes her when she plays the outraged queen although she is actually nothing but a spoiled baby.

A baby who now has a baby, one that lives far away in Ivujivik at a cousin's house, but who, through no fault of his own, will always serve as a weapon whenever his mother needs one. Elsewhere in the world, there are child soldiers, but you have baby bombs, baby machine guns, baby bear traps. A baby in the arms of a sixteen-year-old child who is mad at the world, and especially at Tayara Nassak, a baby aimed like a nuclear missile at his own father, a baby grenade who never actually asked to explode.

2

CECILIA IS GOING TO START school soon. School is always a little scary, but here it's the jungle, a glacial jungle, but the jungle all the same. You have to be strong, know how to return punches, protect those sensitive zones. Cecilia is so gentle and small, she only has sensitive zones. I'm scared they'll pluck her bald like a willow ptarmigan.

Do you remember Jessy? Oh, Jessy. They called him a white boy, and maybe it's true; no one, not even Jessy, ever found out who his father was. Jessy with his fawn eyes. Deer are too fragile for the tundra. They broke him so many times he stopped coming to school. Jessy is afraid of other children the way you are afraid of evil spirits. I don't want them to break Cecilia.

There is so much anger in these little bodies. Lava-spitting volcanoes. Tukka is like a tank in the middle of the schoolyard, with a thousand arms like so many cannons flinging rocks in all directions: a broken windowpane, then another, now three. I ran under these projectiles, dove upon the tank, but there was nothing I could do. We had to get his grandmother to make it stop. The grandmothers here can calm down all kinds of storms. They take care of their grandchildren while the parents have better things to do, for sure. They are the comfy nests covered in eiderdown, they are the igloos that miraculously appear in the middle of family blizzards, when mommies and daddies are fighting.

The grandmothers still know how to catch fish and gut them. The floors of their houses are covered in cardboard where they lay their catch, where they cut away beluga skin to make the *mattaq* that the rest of the family will enjoy. Or else they pluck willow ptarmigan, or skin foxes. There's always bannock and black tea ready in their kitchens; they lovingly sew coats to wrap each of their many grandchildren in. They rock the babies when their mothers have had too much to drink. The grandmothers are the ones left holding the children, and they hold the villages together too, from one end of the tundra to the other.

And when they disappear, it's a catastrophe. Jessy's grandmother went to Montreal for cancer treatments and now nobody is taking care of him. His mother says she doesn't want him anymore; his big sister doesn't want him either. Often grandmothers are children's only hope, but cancer doesn't care.

.

Nobody calls Tukka white. To them, he's a nigger. There are more and more of those kids these days with lovely milk chocolate skin and slightly almond-shaped eyes. For a few years now, some Haitians from Montreal North have landed on the construction sites. Once a year, Tukka and the others go to Montreal to see their dads. Sometimes their mom takes advantage of the occasion to make them a new little brother, but sometimes she doesn't.

Fred watches TV, squished in the middle of the couch between two guys from the Lower St. Lawrence. Tukka, quiet now, rides by the camp on his little bicycle. The Lower St. Lawrence guys laugh.

Another one of yours, Fred? Wow, you really are a productive sort of guy. Seems I've seen at least four or five since we arrived. Unless it's the same one. They're all the same anyway. You're such a fucking pervert. We know, with that huge cock of yours...

Fred has a wife he loves, and two kids as black as he is. He has never touched a woman up here, but he doesn't say a word, even though he knows he is far from being the biggest pervert on the couch.

3

YOU COME HERE to steal our jobs.

Adamie is the one who says it. Who spits in my face one morning when I have the misfortune of being white in his presence. Standing on the front steps of City Hall, we have a great view of the houses on the shore of the bay, houses to be rebuilt or built, houses brimming with activity from morning to night, white men everywhere, on roofs, on front steps, inside walls.

"Do you see any Inuit? Do you see ANY Inuit?"

Adamie rages like a blizzard two inches from my face, angrily gestures toward the construction sites with a large, wild wave of his long, skinny arms. Adamie's face is emaciated from a never-ending winter.

Salluit. "Skinny people." When your ancestors settled here, thousands of years ago, they were promised more game than they would know what to do with, caribou in the tundra grazing as far as the eye could see, seals and ptarmigan too fat to escape when they approached, belugas leaping up into their kayaks. But there wasn't anything here, nothing to fill their empty stomachs, nothing for their crying kids, nothing for the wives who carried them.

Today the famines are a thing of the distant past, but your whole body remembers. Hunger is written in your blood, in your bones. The kids sitting around the table in the school kitchen wait for their snacks. You can't ever leave food anywhere without supervision, or they will pounce upon it like wolves and they won't leave any, not a crumb; they'll just devour everything in a few minutes, devour a whole summer's worth of provisions. Your bodies have forgotten nothing. You are hungry and you are insatiable.

Adamie resents me for stealing his job even though I hardly know how to hold a hammer. He would kick me out of his village right now, with all the other white people, all aboard a plane and *don't come back no more* and I don't know how to tell him that *we* dream of seeing them everywhere too; on the construction sites, at the school, in the medical clinic, in the government offices, everywhere.

But Adamie, all the Inuit I hire let me down, one after the other.

4

NOBODY STOLE your job from you, Elijah. What they took from you was far more precious.

He arrived in the spring, like the others. He came from a little village in Portneuf. Those construction guys are like homesick soldiers: they tell each other stories about their villages, pride and affection shining in their eyes, delighted when they happen to meet someone who knows their little area, the little place where they come from. After a month or two they have ten days off and they go home like young lieutenants on leave.

His name was Félix. He was maybe thirty-five, maybe a bit younger. He rarely spoke, but he smiled a lot. He had a loud laugh. He had a few days of stubble on his face. A few grey hairs were beginning to appear at his temples. Grey eyes, or blue; it depended on the day and on the colour of his jacket. He was staying at a Makivik camp.

When fresh meat arrives in town, people can smell it. The girls watch the new arrivals and fight over their favourites. But not all of them. Some of them don't care. Maata didn't care, and neither did Félix. Maybe that's how they got together.

Maata had grown up alongside Cecilia. She had reached the age of twenty but still looked like a little fairy, a poor, hard-working fairy bent over her math books until late at night. While the others were partying, she was working hard to finish high school. In the meantime, she supported herself by working weekends in the kitchen of a construction camp with her friend Mary. Maata, the quiet mouse, Mary the loud laugher, both helped Rémi, the head chef, a strange sort of Frenchman who had somehow ended up in their village at the end of the world. The construction guys would try to peer over the counters to see the generous curve of Mary's breasts as she leaned over the dishes, watch her plump rear end dart from the stove to the sink to the fridge, imagine grabbing hold of her wide hips right there, surrounded by the enticing aroma of shepherd's pie.

Happiness came easily to Mary; she responded to all of life's little pleasures with an overflow of joy: the leftover blueberry pie that Rémi let her take home, a ride in the young plumber's pickup, a deserted road going far up the mountain, the young plumber with the half-closed eyes, his face wedged between her breasts. It was a while before the guys took any notice of Maata; most of the time, she was hidden behind the enormous pile of vegetables she was peeling.

.

Félix had never been one to watch TV. In May, when the nights started arriving later, he filled the interminable days with long walks on roads that lengthen with every year, at the edges of the village. Progress at work: every summer when we come back, the airplane flies over Salluit and it's a shock—the village is expanding faster than the most formidable suburbs. More and more new houses, neighbourhoods, more and more spread out, but they can't build them fast enough to keep up with all the babies you produce. The roads keep going deeper and deeper into the mountains. They say that one day the road will go from Salluit all the way to Deception Bay, fifty kilometres to the east. That would make the Raglan mine guys happy; they do so love to dig. Félix kept to the roads. Spring's too-soft snow like icing spread over the tundra.

In May, the village stops sleeping. The kids are outside all night; they climb the piles of boards that Félix will use the next day, but he doesn't say a word. Sometimes he smiles at them. Then the girls come after him, hearing the snow crunching under his boots like a call to them, but he just keeps going. He isn't looking for company. Solitude is precious when you spend all your time, day and night, with a group of forty men.

One evening, he was coming home just as the girls were leaving; they had just finished the dishes. He recognized Mary and her big smile, but he didn't remember having ever noticed Maata. He watched her as she moved away, her head bare despite the cold, her fine black hair against the white fur of her hood. Now Félix too peered over the counter, leaving Mary's generous curves to the plumber and to all the other guys, smiling shyly at Maata whenever he managed to meet her eyes over the enormous pile of potatoes. One night Mary got into her plumber's truck and Maata hurried up to Félix, who was leaving for his walk. She didn't say anything, didn't ask him if he wanted company. They both knew that they wanted to walk together, in silence, in the soft snow.

You wondered which one of them had started it: was it him or her, as if that could change anything, as if that would hurt you less. But it will break your heart whatever happened, Elijah. It's not her, it's not him; they simply walked a lot and spoke very little, that night and the following ones. When Maata wasn't at work, Félix took a detour to go by her house. The whole village saw them walking together, and so did you. In the spring, the night refuses all discretion. And once more, they all started to whisper behind your back.

.

In June, Félix beat the plumber to the keys to the truck. They left for the mountain hollow; all the young people make love in trucks in the mountain hollow; it's the only place that offers any privacy. None of you can even dream of a bedroom of your own where you can wrap your arms around your lover.

To each their exotic fantasies: white people dream of an embrace on a moss bed in the tundra, under the Northern Lights. The Inuit dream of a big comfy bed in a quiet, clean, nicely decorated room.

As Félix placed his lips on Maata's, tenderly holding her chin between his fingers, brushing her hair away from her nape, you waited for her to come back, watching from the window in the living room where her family pretended to be absorbed by an American reality show. Cecilia was fast asleep.

5

SHE CAME HOME LATE. On foot. She didn't want you to see her get out of the truck. She lay down next to her sister in the big bed in the middle of the living room. She pretended not to see you sitting there in the dark, in a corner of the kitchen.

Two days later, Félix went away on vacation. You hoped he would never come back. He did though, just in time to see the ice breaking up. They climbed to the top of the cliff together to admire the show. The ice had been cracking everywhere for a while now. Even so, kids were still speeding back and forth on snowmobiles, from one end of the bay to the other. It started cracking louder. It started to rumble and roar, revolting against the winter and its prison of ice. The fjord gathered up all its courage and split the ice all at once. The water sprang up in a fury, everywhere, and the vengeful current carried the broken pieces of ice far away as the waves celebrated their freedom for Félix and Maata's benefit.

They moved away from the cliff's edge, found a little hollow hidden by the rocks, spread out an old sleeping bag. They embraced each other, with more heat this time, to forget the cold air.

You wondered which one of them had started it: was it him or her, as if that could change anything, as if that would hurt you less, you who'd had to share her once, you wondered why she wanted someone else again, and especially why a white man.

White people are unfair competition. They don't have to be good-looking to take your women; the paleness of their skin is enough of an attraction. They represent the possibility of another place, an elsewhere, another life, a little happiness, maybe.

6

Rémi watches Maata blush as Félix comes to get his plate. The Breton has been around long enough to have seen plenty of white men help themselves to a little interlude with women who will love them too much.

Rémi doesn't say anything, never asks any questions. He greets everyone warmly, smiles when asked what he is doing so far from home, but never answers. Rémi makes a mockery of beaten paths. He's an improbable trajectory, one of those uncontrollable stars that appear here and there in the Northern sky.

He's kind of like Miguel, who was born in Peru to Chinese parents, immigrated to Canada; first to Vancouver, then to Montreal, an artist-in-residence at the end of the world. Miguel's Asian features make him pass as an Inuk, but he dreams in Cantonese, and sometimes in Spanish. Or like Dara, born in Cambodia, moved to Quebec at the age of eighteen, back in Salluit every summer to help keep things organized at the Co-op. Dara prepares sushi and sesame tartar with Arctic char, the taste of the North blending with Cambodian spices. Or Victor, the Cameroonian math teacher; Ahmed, the Algerian science teacher; Dean, the Tanzanian English teacher; Jamie, the Jamaican social worker.

.

Rémi likes to walk on the pier. It doesn't look like Brittany, but it's still the sea. Newly unloaded containers lined up like sentinels of the tundra. The children jump from one to the other, as usual, the children in their own little children's world with its intricate rules. The children here are used to managing by themselves, probably why they hardly ever listen to the adults.

Rémi hears a rock whistle by his ear. He doesn't have to turn around to know that it's Saami who threw it. Saami does that a lot. Most of the guys who work at Makivik dream of giving that kid a good wallop, the little brat. Saami throws rocks, breaks windows, keys trucks. He steals materials, insults people for fun, destroys everything he can. At night in the construction camps, a lot of people dream of getting their hands on him, but not Rémi. Rémi has never dreamed of hitting anyone.

Rémi keeps going and then lingers under the boat hangar. He waits. When Saami goes by, Rémi lets him get ahead, and then he follows him. This isn't the first time. When the night stopped arriving, back in May, Rémi got used to walking around the village very early in the morning, before making breakfast for the guys.

One day he went by Saami's house. The guys would have been happy; the little brat was getting a good thrashing. Rémi threw himself against this freezer chest of a man who was digging his feet into Saami's ribs, and pushed him with all his might. The giant crumbled, immediately sank to the ground. Passed-out drunk. Saami got up without a word and went into his house. He didn't say thank you, he threw rocks, but Rémi doesn't care; he goes by the house every evening, just in case.

7

SPRING IS NEVER EASY for you, Elijah. It hasn't been easy for five years. It's never easy to see the ice melt and free space in the fjord, space in which to throw another body. A body can slide in so easily between two blocks of ice; it gently slips into the water, under the ice; it disappears without leaving a trace. The raging spring currents carry it far away to where it will never be found.

She knew. She knew that every spring you hear your mother's voice scream louder than the roar of the ice. She knew that this year you would get into your canoe again with painful impatience. She knew that you would disappear for a few days to look for ghosts until you came back to your senses. She knew and yet she turned her back on you, during the spring thaw; she was nibbling on another man's neck. And you, you saw thousands of women floating between the blocks of ice, like every year when the banks of the fjord crumble, but for the first time, Maata wasn't there with you.

She came home later. She smelled like wet earth. You were like a dog begging to be petted. You wanted to cry. It's the spring thaw, and my mother is dead. You are the only one here to love me, and my daughter, if she's mine. Pet me, stroke my hair, stroke me please. It's meltdown time. But like all the men of the North, you didn't say anything. You both pretended nothing was going on. You left early the next morning for your annual pilgrimage, and she didn't say a word.

8

IT'S LOUD IN A CONSTRUCTION camp. Men say women are big talkers, but they're a lot worse. Félix hardly ever speaks, but the others make up for him.

In any case, she's gotta be pretty fucking tight. Does she give good head? She looks so shy, but sometimes those ones are the best, the wildest in bed. You did okay, Félix, got a nice piece of ass there. And at least she's still got all of her teeth. You know, that doesn't always come with the territory around here.

Félix eats in silence. He keeps the sweet details to himself. He has no desire to display Maata's body in words, or to discuss the tenderness of their embraces. The less he speaks, the more the others do it for him. They look behind the counter to check out the size of Maata's breasts, her hips, her rear end. They haven't yet understood that a woman is not a sum of parts, but a whole; they like their sex mathematical.

Félix never says much, whether he is in the North or the South, either to men or women. Maata would like to know a little bit more about him; she would especially like to know if she is the only one. But he doesn't say anything, his hands speak for him, his hands say *you're the one I want*, they say *you are beautiful*, they say *I love you*, but she longs for his mouth to say it too.

9

CECILIA CAN'T SLEEP. She is thinking about the whore. She doesn't know what that is, but she is sure that it's not a princess. She doesn't believe it's an animal either. She is pretty sure it's not something that is pretty or nice. Saami is the one who said it, and Saami never says anything nice.

Your mother's a whore.

It was earlier that day, sometime in the middle of the afternoon. Cecilia was playing with Ruusie, Saami's little sister, outside their house. Saami had just woken up. When you spend your nights being the king of the containers at the marina, you sleep during the day. He went out on the porch, saw Cecilia, and uttered his first words of the day.

"Your mother's a whore."

He smiled his obnoxious, smug little smile and returned inside. Cecilia hasn't dared ask anyone yet, not her father or her grandmother, especially not her mother. She doesn't see her mother much these days. She works a lot and comes home late. Like right now, she hasn't come home yet. Cecilia gets up, makes her invisible way behind the sofa upon which the rest of the family is crammed together. They are mesmerized by the television and don't notice her. Her father is drinking out of a bottle. Cecilia slips on her rubber boots and goes out in her pyjamas. She walks toward the camp, a little zombie in pyjamas featuring kittens. She walks without paying attention to the little swarms of children that she passes through, dozens of little processions of runaway children. They are running away from all kinds of things. They spend their nights outside because life is so much easier there than at home. She walks toward the camp. She comes closer. A few men are smoking cigarettes outside. They think she is an apparition, a spirit in pink pyjamas, a ghost sent by the children they planted in the tundra. They make jokes and laugh nervously. She stands in front of them. She doesn't say a word. The men don't know what to do. They squirm uncomfortably. They feel guilty but she doesn't say a word against them. Someone murmurs something about those irresponsible people who don't take care of their kids. It doesn't matter. Cecilia doesn't understand French. Someone says that she might be one of the employees' daughters. Someone goes to get Rémi.

Rémi recognizes Cecilia, kneels before her, tenderly strokes her hair. He knows that Maata has left. He doesn't know when she is coming back. He takes Cecilia by the hand and brings her inside, settles her at one of the tables, deserted at this hour. He finds her some paper and some pencils. Cecilia doesn't feel like drawing. She doesn't move. Rémi doesn't either. They wait in silence.

The gravel creaks under the weight of the returning truck. The doors slam. Cecilia listens; she recognizes her mother's light footsteps as they move away. She leaps up and runs to the door, flings it open, walks right into Félix, who is about to come in, her head colliding with his belly. They look at each other. Félix's eyes are two headlights in the darkness and Cecilia is the deer caught in them. Blinded and paralyzed by fear, she finally manages to pull her eyes away from Félix's and runs to join her mother. Maata swoops her daughter up and continues home. Cecilia instantly falls asleep in her arms.

In his narrow bed, Félix can't sleep. He has a daughter too.

10

THEY HAVE WANDERED far from the village. They followed the road that might, one day, go all the way to the mine. Félix asks her what her daughter's name is.

Cecilia.

Félix finds that pretty. He thinks of the Simon and Garfunkel song. Maata doesn't know it. He sings it to her. He wishes he had his guitar. He stops singing. He tells her that he has a daughter too. Laura. She is older than Cecilia; she'll be ten next summer. Maata holds her breath. She wants him to keep talking. But he kisses her, and gently begins to unzip her hoodie. It's okay. Maata is patient. His hands tell her that he loves her.

He has taken his jacket off, it's lying on the back seat. His nose is in her hair, he can't see a thing, but Maata can see very well. She sees his wallet, which is falling out of his jacket pocket. She caresses the nape of his neck with her left hand and stretches her right toward the jacket. She grabs the wallet and manages to push it under the seat. She slips her right hand under Félix's t-shirt.

Later, they come back to the village. Félix leaves her at the camp, as usual. He doesn't notice that she lingers in the truck for a few seconds before opening the door. She bids him good night and goes away, her heart beating fast. She hides in the shack. She opens the wallet. She looks at his driver's license. He is thirty-three. He has credit cards and a hundred dollars in cash but she isn't interested in that. She is looking for photographs. She finds two. There's a little girl who has his eyes. There is a woman who has the little girl's smile. She consoles herself with the thought that the photo doesn't seem to be very recent.

She retraces her steps. She throws the wallet on the ground next to the truck, driver's side.

11

FIRST OF JULY. It's Canada Day, which you celebrate up here, but you're not in the mood. You came along anyway. Maata has drawn a red maple leaf on Cecilia's cheek. You arrived together, like a family. You brought some cans of Budweiser. Maata doesn't drink; you drink for both of you.

There are so many people. You're overwhelmed. The music is loud: country music in Inuttitut. The Canadian flag is stencilled onto the folding chairs. Old wooden pallets, picked up from the construction sites, feed a large campfire. There are no trees, so no logs.

You walk a bit, say hi to some cousins, a few friends. You don't see any *Qallunaat*. You relax a little. You have nothing to fear, Elijah. The Québécois from the South don't often feel like celebrating this particular holiday, but you can't know that; you've never thought of yourself as Québécois: you're Canadian, like most of the Inuit. You listen to English music, watch English movies and English television programs.

You look at Maata. You wonder if she's disappointed. You search for the answer on her face, but you can't read anything on her smooth skin. You let her talk to her friends. You slowly walk away from the party. Ahead of you, a girl is reeling. You pass her and then notice it's Aleisha. You stop. She's had a lot to drink; you, not that much. You walk along together.

"I can't find Tayara. I'm sure he's gone to the mountain with Maggie. Fucking skank. I hate that fucking bitch. The slut.

Do you wanna come with me? We'll find her and smash her fucking face in.

You follow Aleisha. The two of you make your halting, teetering way up the mountain. You pass the can of Budweiser back and forth. Nobody's there. You let yourselves drop down on some rocks. Aleisha brings her face close to yours.

"We should get back at them. We should do the same thing to them. You shouldn't let those guys fuck you over either."

You kiss. You have the impression that Aleisha is going to devour you. She pushes her tongue deep in your mouth, bites you, grabs your short hair. You put your hand inside her jacket, stroke her breasts under her tank top. Her breasts are bigger than Maata's. It feels weird. She pushes you onto your back, undoes your belt, pulls down your pants, takes you in her mouth. You feel a strange tightening in your chest. You push her away, get up, put your pants back on.

"Hey, what's the matter with you? Where are you going? Hey, what's wrong with you? What the hell is your fucking problem? Are you a faggot, is that it? Poor Maata. I understand why she has no choice but to fuck her white guy."

You're not listening anymore. You've already left.

12

FIRST OF JULY. Félix walks up to the telephone and takes out his calling card. They all have the same expression, the construction guys, when they take out those cards and walk up to a phone. They aren't big, virile men anymore; they're homesick little boys.

Félix dials the number he knows by heart, holds his breath as he counts the rings—one, two, three—and Maude answers. She asks how he's doing, in a happy voice. She asks if it is still very light out. She asks if he manages to sleep. He wishes he could tell her that, no, he can't sleep, because he misses her, but he tells her instead that you get used to these too-bright nights. He tells her about the midnight sun because she loves that; his stories transport her into another world. He knows that right now she must be squinting, as if the tundra were superimposed on the wheat fields outside her house.

She passes the phone to Laura. His heart leaps as he hears his daughter's fluty voice. He listens with his eyes closed. He thinks of a swallow; his daughter is a little swallow. A moment of joy. He wishes her a good night. He says, "Give me your mother." She gives the telephone back to Maude.

"I miss you, Maude."

She doesn't answer. Not immediately. They breathe together.

"Félix…"

He hangs up. He can't take that apologetic tone of hers. He doesn't want to hear the rest: that they'd been too young back then, that he has always been a good father, that she likes him a lot. He wants her to love him. He doesn't want to hear that she hopes he'll find the right woman some day. She's the one, and she knows it. He shoves his calling card back in his wallet and goes to bed.

13

LOW TIDE. She wasn't working. She invited Félix to meet her after supper. She told him not to eat too much.

She waits on the wharf with plastic buckets. They walk away from the marina. The bay is still. The sun smashes over the cliffs. The cliffs become giddy, they glisten. You can smell the sea. Salluit is just stunning, as beautiful as Norway.

They stamp their feet in the mud and in a few inches of water, plunge their hands in the freezing water to pull up rocks, throw handfuls of mussels into their pails. These mussels are tiny, nothing like their cousins from the South, as if their tininess protected them from the cold water.

Félix grew up in the forest, doesn't know the sea. He's happy, like a kid at Old Orchard Beach. Maata opens a shell and swallows a mussel raw. Félix watches her. She smiles at him, breaks another shell, holds the mollusk out to him with laughing eyes. He hesitates for a second before closing his teeth on it. He likes it. They laugh. His hands are frozen; she puts them under her sweater. She opens a third mussel and delicately places its flesh on Félix's tongue.

That's when you got there, at precisely that moment. You appeared from above, from the top of the boulders. They didn't see you coming. You cast your line in the water, without a word. Félix waves at you. You give him a curt nod. He abandons his bucket at Maata's feet and goes over to you. He asks you a thousand questions. He wants to know everything: what you are trying to catch, the best place to catch a fish, whether you have a boat, who taught you how to fish. As soon as you gather enough courage to answer a question he immediately asks you another. You can't do this. You just wish he would stop talking.

Maata keeps collecting mussels with amazing efficiency. Soon both pails are full. She leaves them next to Félix: "Give these to Rémi. He'll take care of them."

She leaves. Félix looks surprised, but he keeps asking you questions. He finally asks you what your name is.

"Elijah."

He says his name is Félix, but you know that.

14

IT'S AS IF RÉMI just won the lottery. He drags Félix into the kitchen. He empties their booty into the sink and assigns Félix the task of cleaning. He opens the crammed refrigerator, sticks his arm all the way to the back and pulls it back out, triumphantly grasping a bottle of white wine. "For emergencies."

He whistles as he prepares the sauce. He's a Breton cooking mussels, and he's happy. It smells so good that they worry that the others will show up and demand some. They eat out of the bucket, smiles on their lips. Félix asks Rémi if he knows someone called Elijah.

"Yeah, that's Maata's boyfriend."

Félix wonders aloud if Elijah managed to catch any fish. Rémi pretends not to notice that Félix is blushing.

15

THE PLUMBER TOOK THE TRUCK. Félix and Maata left on foot to find a quiet spot in the tundra. They sit on a boulder. Maata leans her head on Félix's shoulder, her nose in his beard. She wishes they could just stay like this forever, if only they could stay exactly like this, the horizon ending at the tip of her nose. She doesn't want to see any farther than Félix's beard. The rough cloth of his jacket is a bit itchy under her chin but that doesn't stop her from wishing she could just stay right there, forever. Félix strokes her hand and then slides his hand under her face, gently pulls his shoulder away so that he can look at her.

"You didn't tell me. About Elijah."

And you didn't tell me about the girl in your wallet, she wants to shout. Do you still love her, are you going back to her when you leave, is she prettier than me, do you prefer white girls? She wishes she could scream all of this, but she stays calm, like the bay; she hides her storms under the July sun. She says it doesn't matter. "About Elijah. It doesn't matter. It's not a big deal."

"I think it's a big deal. I know what it is to love a girl who is with someone else."

Maata waits for what happens next. But nothing does. Maata hopes with all her heart that the girl in the wallet loves someone else.

16

Tayara Nassak adores spy movies. He's seen quite a few, but this time, he's the hero. He bought his ticket three days ago without telling anyone about it. He sacrificed two hundred dollars for a ten-ounce bottle of Smirnoff. He went by Aleisha's late that evening. They went into the bedroom and closed the door, and before she started screaming, he took out the vodka and the hyena turned into a kitten, instantly.

She took a big gulp, smiled, and rolled on top of him. They took off their clothes as she continued to drink. She was sweet and gentle and nice; she didn't wail at him. Tayara looked at the bottle and wondered what it had that he lacked. When they were finished, he lay spooning her, stroking her with one hand as he moved the bottle toward her mouth at regular intervals. She faded into sleep. He withdrew from her, put his clothes back on and left without a sound. He went back home, packed his suitcase and sat on it. He didn't dare move, for fear of falling asleep or changing his mind. He left at 6 o'clock. He ran into his little sister and told her to let their parents know. He went over to his friend Steevie's house, across the street, the living room filled with smoke and empty bottles, as usual. Steevie was still up, though glassy-eyed, busy with Candy Crush: "I need a lift to the airport." Steevie got up, and after a moment, found the keys to the truck amongst the trash on the table. They went to Tayara's to get his suitcase and then took off for the airport. As they were going up the hill, Tayara watched as the village got farther and farther away, wondering when he would be back.

Now he is sitting in the nearly empty waiting room. He anxiously watches the door, as if staring at it would stop Aleisha from suddenly appearing, shouting her head off. Stop her from throwing herself on him, scratching him, biting him, tearing his clothes. But Aleisha doesn't come, and he gets onto the plane. He made it. He's left. He's going to Montreal and he's going to be a superstar, fuck Salluit, he is going to make it all the way to L.A. and he'll have all the girls he wants, all those black sluts in those music videos. He will fuck them all and they won't dare scream at him. He'll have a big fat revolver and he'll command respect with that gun, and with his cock.

17

ALEISHA WAKES UP with a huge headache, the almost-empty bottle taunting her at the foot of her bed. She takes a shower. She feels like a slushie; she tells herself that it would do her some good. She walks towards the Northern. She returns home, calmly, sipping her tropical punch, she who has never seen a palm tree. She runs into Steevie, who asks her when Tayara will be back. He says he forgot to ask him that this morning. She doesn't understand, so he repeats, "How long is he going to stay in Montreal?" She drops her slushie, runs to Tayara's house. She wants to kill him, but he isn't there. She runs into his little sister.

"Tayara went to Montreal. He doesn't know when he'll be back."

Aleisha trembles. She absolutely has to know when he will be back. She repeats, louder and louder, "When? When? When? When?" His little sister shrugs her shoulders. Aleisha slaps her and leaves, crying. And she cries for days, drinks for days, and she wails to the whole world that she will kill herself. She won't: here, there are those who say they will, and those who do it.

18

TAYARA DRINKS TOO. It's so easy here. Montreal is great, man.

So easy. I want a beer, and it's right there. It costs, like, nothing, almost nothing, and I don't have to hide because I'm afraid someone's gonna steal it. It's so easy. Montreal is great, man, I fucking love it.

He has been drinking since he got off the plane, it's so easy. Easy to take the airport shuttle downtown, downtown with its thousands of bars; the hardest thing is to choose one, but Tayara didn't bother choosing, he just went to the first one he saw. He just sat down and drank.

I don't fucking care, these people think I drank too much— Tayara left the bar just before he was about to get kicked out— *but I don't fucking care.*

He wandered about in the sticky July heat. He walked around drunkenly in a city where for once he had the luxury of not knowing a soul. He walked until his legs stopped and he collapsed onto a park bench. He slept a little, his head on his suitcase.

In the morning he remembered the crumpled piece of paper in the pocket of his jeans. Annie's name and address. Annie was his mother's cousin who he had only seen once or twice. She left Salluit long before his birth. She found some kind of white person job somewhere in the South and she's hardly ever gone home. Sometimes for funerals, when she has the time; she works a lot.

Dorval. He has no idea where that is. He thinks about it. He thinks that might be where the airport is. He tells himself that he has to retrace his footsteps, but his feet have gone in so many directions that he doesn't know where he has to go back to. He hails a taxi, gets in and hands the driver the slip of paper.

The car is air-conditioned. The fresh air feels good, but he is still a little nauseated. The driver stops in front of a beige and brown bungalow, in the middle of a street that is completely still and filled with beige and brown bungalows. Tayara pays and drags himself and his suitcase up to the door.

A woman in pyjamas opens the door. She takes in his glassy eyes and his boozy breath, but she lets him in. She settles him on a futon in the basement, tells him there are towels in the bathroom and stuff to eat in the fridge. She tells him she's got to go to work, but he doesn't care, he's already asleep. Annie silently watches him sleep. And inside her head, she screams. She will never escape, she knows, despite the thousands of kilometres, she's still there, with a drunk man passed out on her couch.

19

MAATA WOKE UP EARLY. She stayed still, listening. She wanted to hear the plane take off, but she fell back asleep. She opened her eyes again at nine o'clock, and it was too late. Félix must have already flown by Kangiqsujuaq.

She gets up, rummages around in her school notebooks until she finds her map of Quebec. She puts her finger on her village, softly traces the outlines of the province, slides from Ungava Bay all the way to Kuujjuaq, then crosses the interminable distance to Quebec City, at the bottom of the map. He isn't going to Montreal, he told her; he lives "in a little village not too far from Quebec City". She has never been to Quebec City. He told her it was pretty, that it looked like Europe, but she has never been to Europe either. She wonders if she knows enough things for him, if she has seen enough places. She hears the white people talk; they always have so many things to say. She has nothing to say. She just wishes she could tell him she loves him, but she doesn't dare.

He left for ten days. He went to see his little girl, who will turn ten tomorrow, ten days for ten years. Maata wishes someone could unplug her for ten days, wishes she could just sleep until his return, don't talk to me, wake me up when he comes back. But it won't work. Cecilia comes to her and tells her she's hungry. Maata serves her a bowl of cereal. Maata is quite sure he will also see the woman in the wallet, she wonders if he will touch the woman the way he touches her; it hurts her to think of things like that. She wishes she could stop thinking for ten days.

20

IT TOOK YOU A WHILE, but you finally decided to go there, walking with slow steps, your hands in the pockets of your kangaroo jacket. You went to the camp on your tiptoes, like a kid arriving late at school. It was somewhere in the middle of the morning. The days when you manage to wake up before the afternoon, you have more courage. You take advantage of that to accomplish your delicate missions.

Rémi greeted you with a big smile, as usual, and he told you that Maata wasn't working that day. You knew that, it's why you had come, but you didn't explain that to Rémi. He offered you toast with peanut butter. You sat on the counter to eat your snack. Rémi watched you eat and you remembered those mornings in the school kitchen, at breakfast with the other empty-bellied kids, under the gaze of the teachers who took turns serving you. The empty-bellied kids on the school doorstep long before eight o'clock, before the kitchen opened, up with the tremulous winter dawn, waiting for a bowl of cereal.

You thought of Cecilia, you wondered if you and Maata had always made her breakfast, but you couldn't remember. You thanked Rémi and asked him if you could see Félix.

"He's on vacation in the South for ten days."

Ten days. A reprieve. You weren't expecting that, but the knot in your stomach loosened a little. A ten-day reprieve.

You left as Rémi was wondering if he should warn Félix, wondering if you were looking for Félix because you wanted to send a bullet into his skull or simply talk to him. We never can tell which it will be up here. You didn't know either, didn't really know why you wanted to see Félix. You wanted to stand in front of him, stand with your head up, your back straight, without trembling. You didn't want him to remember you as some poor jerk barely capable of putting two sentences together. He had surprised you at the marina. Now it was your turn to surprise him on his territory.

You went home. Cecilia was riding her tricycle in front of the house. Maata was sitting with her notebooks open, her mind obviously elsewhere. You closed your bedroom door. You wanted to be tender, so tender. You stroked her face, you kissed her neck. You dragged her to the bed, you took off her clothes and yours, you lay down on top of her. She was lying on her back obediently, gazing toward the window. You stopped, you put on your clothes and you left. You didn't slam the door.

You walked over to Aleisha's house. She was still sleeping, knocked out by all she had drunk the night before. You slipped into her bedroom, undressed, slipped into bed beside her. You caressed her with the tenderness that Maata hadn't wanted. Aleisha smiled, her eyes closed, pulled you to her. You made love, both dreaming of another.

21

JULY ENDS TODAY. It's Laura's birthday. She is ten years old and she is magnificent, full of joy and life. Félix feels like being happy too, feels like being happy the way you can be happy when you're ten years old and it's a beautiful summer day and there's an enormous chocolate cake in front of you.

Félix feels like being happy even if Maude invited François or Francis, he never remembers his name; he doesn't want to remember either him or his name. He's there today, but Félix doesn't care. He just feels like being happy.

The day ends with children's laughter and splashes in the pool; the day gradually slides into a warm evening, and the guests all leave except for François or Francis, of course. Félix asks Laura if she wants to go camping at the lake, and she's ready in less than two minutes. Maude asks her to go wait for her father in the car.

Félix looks at Maude, who looks at François or Francis. Félix tries to remember what François or Francis does for a living, apart from being his wife's lover. Félix can't remember whether he's an accountant or a plumber. His head obstinately refuses to retain the tiniest bit of information about the guy. Maude looks at Félix. "I'm pregnant." She keeps talking, but Félix can't hear anything anymore. He sees her lips move but no sound is coming out. He calmly walks toward the door. He sees Maude in front of him, moving her head and her arms and her hands, but he still doesn't hear anything. He goes outside and walks toward his car. Maude grabs his arm: "Maybe I should hang onto Laura tonight, you look like you're in a state of shock, maybe she should stay with me…."

Félix gently pulls his arm away. He gets behind the wheel, smiles at Laura and they go off to roast wieners and count the stars above the lake.

22

IT'S FIVE IN THE MORNING. Someone is knocking at the door. Annie is awake, hasn't slept the past three nights. Tayara hasn't been home for three nights now. She has spent three nights wondering if he has been stabbed in an alley. Three days and three nights vacillating between loathing and worry.

Annie is afraid she'll see a police car outside her house, police officers at her door, crows, messengers of death. She opens the curtains. She sees a car parked in the alley, but it's only a taxi. She answers the door. Tayara stands tottering, in front of her. "Can you pay the cab driver? I don't have any money left," he says. Before she can answer he staggers towards the stairs to the basement. She catches him before he falls headfirst down the steps. She makes him sit down in the living room. She pays the driver. Tayara is fast asleep when she returns. He smells like rotten walrus.

23

AUGUST. FÉLIX IS BACK TODAY; you saw him get out of the truck with his travel bag, but you didn't dare talk to him. Maata was at work, you thought she'd be home late tonight but you don't care, you haven't touched her for ten days now. You prefer to go to Aleisha's; you clasp each other in fury, with the rage of the spurned. It is like rolling in flames, it is ecstasy.

Maata hurries to finish the dishes. Mary watches her, smiling.

"Calm down, baby." (She pronounces it *come* down.) "Don't worry. Take your time. We'll leave you the truck."

Maata blushes, the glass slips from her hands but she manages to catch it before it falls. She hurries. She goes to the truck. Félix is waiting for her. They take the road that will go all the way to the mine one day. They stop. Maata's skin tenses, she leans forward a touch. She wishes she could leave her rib cage to get closer to him. She waits. She aches for him to place his hands on her, but his hands don't come. Félix looks ahead, stares at the river, which shrinks, bit by bit, up to the end of the horizon. Maata wants to fall upon him like an *uppik* on a lemming, but she doesn't dare. Women wait for men to touch them, that's the way it is here; the women are the lemmings and the men the birds of prey. She controls herself, holds on tight to her lust, denies her voracious appetite free rein. Holds on tight. She waits, but his hands don't come. She softly slides her hand on Félix's thigh. He gives her a smile that says he is sorry.

.

Aleisha uses all her strength to wind herself around Elijah, all the strength in her arms and legs. She screams with pleasure so that the whole house can hear her, and yes, the neighbours too—why not the whole village. She wants her orgasm to be heard all the way to Montreal. She wants all her friends to know that Elijah is a much better fuck than Tayara. In the next room, the little sisters are giggling, their ears pressed against the wall. They sneak up to Aleisha's bedroom door, laughing. They push it open, the width of one eye; they jostle each other as they take turns watching Elijah's bum between Aleisha's legs, his pelvis going back and forth. They run away shrieking, throwing themselves on their beds, the older ones copying the movements they've just seen, the youngest one choking with laughter.

Cecilia can't sleep. She gets up, crosses the deserted living room. She wants a glass of milk. She looks in all the rooms but nobody's there. She climbs up on the counter, opens the cupboard, clasps a glass in her little hands. The glass is heavier than she thought it would be. It slides from her hands and shatters on the ground. She gets down on the floor and crouches, fascinated by the sparkling shards, and picks one up in her fingers. She takes a step backward, treads on one of the shards and cuts her foot. It bleeds. She sits on the floor in the middle of the kitchen and waits.

24

THE TRUCK IS ALREADY BACK. Rémi is surprised. Félix appears, looking tired, but he smiles as he spots the cook, asks him to wait a second. He returns, handing Rémi a package wrapped in brown paper. A bottle of Ricard. Rémi takes out a couple of glasses. Félix takes a sip, but he prefers beer. Rémi isn't the kind of person to give advice. He hesitates: "Elijah came by while you were gone. I don't know what he wanted, exactly, but... You know, the guys here are jealous."

Yeah, well, guys are jealous everywhere, Félix wants to say, *I'm* crazy jealous, I'm enraged, my ex is pregnant with her new boyfriend's child and it's breaking my heart. I wish that guy never existed; I'm like the Inuit, I would love to take them down with my .12 gauge, but I hold back for my daughter's sake, I guess, for my ex as well because I still love her, idiot that I am. We are the same as the Inuit, poor Rémi, you just don't know it yet. But Félix doesn't say any of that, just mumbles to Rémi not to worry, that he intends to stop seeing Maata. They drink in silence.

Quick knocks at the door. Félix answers. Maata is standing there, holding Cecilia in her arms, the little girl's right foot wrapped in a bandage. She wants to go to the clinic.

Félix doesn't move, finds he can't. The seconds go by slowly. Rémi empties their glasses in the sink, finds a place to hide the bottle, walks up to Félix. "Give me the keys to the truck. I'll go." Maata is disappointed, but she thanks Rémi. Félix wishes them luck and turns away.

25

NOBODY LAUGHS ANYMORE in the kitchen. Maata's eyes are so sad that no one dares joke around. Not Rémi, or Mary, or the construction guys when they come up to get their food. Félix asked how Cecilia was doing. It wasn't anything serious, just a cut. Since then, he hasn't really talked to her anymore, just gives her an awkward smile once in a while.

Maata can't sleep anymore. She walks around outside at night during the few short hours when the sky finally darkens. August, pitiless, marches on towards winter. The other night she saw an aurora borealis, the first of the season, etch its white and timid self on the late summer sky, apologetic as it announced the return of the cold, whispered, sorry, I'm sorry, I'm so sorry.

Maata wants to apologize too, but she doesn't know what she did; she wishes she could turn herself in, go to court and ask what she did. Every time she sees Félix she silently wails *why*, desperate, but only her eyes speak; her mouth doesn't dare to yet.

26

OF COURSE, YOU FOUND OUT as well. You would have liked to be happy about it, to think, well it serves her right and good for you, but it hurt too much to see Maata so sad, there was no room in your heart for joy. You stopped going to Aleisha's. You started getting up in the morning to take care of Cecilia while Maata slept, or pretended to. You clumsily prepared your culinary specialties: eggs, bacon, macaroni. You always saved a generous portion for Maata, even though she ate very little. Sometimes you asked Rémi for cooking tips.

You woke up one night and Maata was crying. You stroked her hair, wiped each tear away with your fingertips, pressed her trembling heart against yours. She lifted her chin toward you, smiled at you, for the first time in weeks. She kissed you on the lips. You made love, tenderly, for the first time in weeks. She fell asleep, for the first time in days. Today you walk toward the docks, with a light heart. You want to bring a fish back for supper. Kids jump, feet together, on top of the containers. You walk by them and a rock grazes your skull. You turn around. Saami sends you a triumphant smile.

"Your girlfriend's a whore."

You drop your fishing rod. You run towards the containers but you have the impression that you are moving in slow motion. You easily climb up to the top. Your fists land on Saami, he collapses, your feet go deep into his sides. People are shouting, but you can't hear anything. You grab Saami by his collar, drag him to the edge, grab him by the legs, his head floating over the rocks. One voice makes its way to your brain, your ears unblock, you can hear again.

"Taima, Elijah. Stop."

It's Rémi. You put down Saami's feet, drag him away from the edge. You get down from your mount, pick up your fishing rod and go home.

27

NOBODY LAUGHS ANYMORE in the kitchen. The whole village is talking about the attack at the marina. Saami's father is promising revenge on Elijah; he's the only one allowed to hit his son.

Maata, impassive, slices carrots. Mary watches her. Mary is Saami's cousin. She goes up to Maata. Maata raises her eyes and tells Mary sharply that she has nothing to do with the fight.

"Come down, baby. I don't want to talk to you about the fight. I want to talk to you about Félix." Maata's heart stops. Félix.

"Patrick talked to him the other day. He knows what happened in the South."

Maata doesn't know who Patrick is, doesn't understand what he has to do with Félix. Mary blushes. Maata guesses. It's the plumber. She puts her knife down, wrings her hands.

"He is still in love with his ex. And his ex is pregnant by her new boyfriend."

Mary wishes she could hug her friend but she moves away, picks up her knife again, silently goes back to slicing carrots. Mary goes back to work too. She hums softly. Maata suddenly drops her knife. "Patrick is the same as all the others. He's going to dump you too, one of these days."

Maata flees to the bathroom.

28

Tayara slept until three in the afternoon. Annie hasn't closed her eyes for even a minute. Tayara takes a shower, throws his clothes in the washing machine, makes himself some eggs.

Annie watches him eat, leaning against the counter. She asks him why he came to Montreal.

"To be a musician."

She asks him what instrument he plays.

"None. I'm a rapper."

She asks him if he has done anything about it yet, met people, made plans. He says he has time. He asks her if she can lend him money for a taxi. She answers that she doesn't have any cash on her. He rummages in his pockets, finds some change, decides to take the bus and the metro.

He gets off at Atwater. He looks for a free spot. Nobody is at the entrance of the shopping centre, it's practically a miracle. He puts his cap on the floor. He hopes it won't take too long. He's thirsty.

29

"Christ, Félix, you were in a better mood when you were fucking your Inuit. Why don't you go get laid, it would do you good. She's dying for it anyway."

He said those words right in front of Maata, convinced that *those people don't understand French anyway.* He found himself hilarious. The others did too; there were five of them, surrounding Félix, roaring with laughter, right under Maata's nose. Maata holds her breath, waiting for the explosion, Félix's fists breaking all five of these idiots' noses, one after the other, but it doesn't happen. Félix isn't Elijah, he doesn't say anything, he gives Maata an apologetic look and just goes away. Mary's filling the plates. She's the one who reacts.

"Motherfuckers."

They understood *that*. Then Mary hissed something else that they didn't understand; those guys don't understand a word of Inuttitut. Mary put down her serving spoons and left with Maata; the guys had to serve themselves.

That night, Patrick came to get Mary in the truck.

"So you want to fuck your Inuit?"

Patrick takes a small step towards her, gently takes her hand.

"We don't have to. We can just go for a walk, look for caribou, or just wait till it gets dark in case there are Northern Lights."

Mary smiles through her tears. She climbs into the truck.

30

MAATA WALKS TOWARDS HER HOUSE. Someone is walking behind her. Someone whispers her name. It's Félix. She wants to ignore him and keep going, wants to get far away, her head up and her back straight. She wants to spit in his face the way he spit in hers, but her feet have a will of their own and they stop; her legs refuse to go forward, her eyes flutter with hope. She's a repentant dog, and she hates herself.

He walks alongside her. They don't speak. They arrive at Maata's house. There's a quad in the yard.

"Is that yours?"

Maata shrugs. Félix wants to go for a ride. Maata enters the house without making a sound, grabs the keys from the table and goes out again to join Félix. She starts the quad. Félix hesitates for a second and then sits down behind her. They leave for the mountains. They drive up to a little camp, a hodgepodge of resourcefulness and scavenged material, stuff salvaged from the "Canadian Tire," as the local dump is affectionately called. A 10x10-foot shack promoted to the rank of cottage: four walls consisting of pieces of plywood patched together, a sloping roof, a door with an actual multi-paned window in it. One of the panes is broken; it's been filled with a piece of cardboard, and that bugs Félix. He wishes he had the necessary tools and stuff to fix it. A chimney extends on the side. Félix is happy to discover a stove. There isn't much wood, just some pieces salvaged from the construction sites, but he lights it anyway. Maata makes tea. They sit next to each other on the mattress that takes up half the space. Félix touches Maata's face with his fingertips. "I'm sorry." They are finally together again. They have missed each other. Night falls, at last. They know it won't last long. They wait for the morning, pressed against each other. At three o'clock, the sky clears and they go back toward the village. Maata goes home, falls asleep in the living room, won't wake up until noon. Félix manages to sleep for an hour before heading back to work.

"So, seems like you got laid. See, it was worth taking my advice!"

Félix doesn't turn around. He lifts his middle finger high in the air and keeps going.

31

THIS TIME ANNIE didn't have to pay for the taxi. He came back on foot, she has no idea how. She let him sleep, take his shower, make himself a sandwich. She pushed her generosity as far as to do his laundry while he slept; she carefully folded everything and put it back in his suitcase, and she carried his bags up to the vestibule. Now he is there, in front of her, devouring his sandwich and Annie prays that she will not lose her nerve. She watches his plate as it empties; she counts the bites he has left before she attacks. She gives herself a reprieve; he has to finish his glass of juice first, a second glass of juice, a third and the bottle is empty. There, he's finished.

"And now, you have to go."

Tayara meets her eyes. He doesn't flinch, and he doesn't say a word. She leans against the counter and keeps going, she tells him to leave, to get a ticket back to Salluit, or to find himself another hotel. She can't take this anymore; he is eating her out of house and home, and taking everything else too, her patience, her sanity. She left the North because she couldn't take drunks in her house anymore but now they have followed her all the way here. Tayara's face becomes strangely blurry as she looks at him and then seems to take on the features of her father, her uncles, her brothers. He gets up; she's trembling. He asks her for money for a taxi; she holds out two twenty-dollar bills without looking at him. He takes them without thanking her and she calls him a cab. He picks up his bag and goes outside to wait on the sidewalk. She collapses on a chair. She watches him from the window until the taxi arrives. She bites her lips until they bleed; her vision is so blurred by tears that she can hardly see him get in the car, hardly see the car disappear around the corner. She puts her head on the kitchen table. She stays there.

32

SEPTEMBER IS HERE. There is a fine dusting of snow on the mountains that surround the village. Flocks of Canada geese cover the clear autumn sky, giving travellers the signal that it is time to go home, and then other birds from the South gradually join them, one at a time. *Nirliit.* Geese.

Patrick left yesterday, went back to his native Gaspésie to spend the winter on the dole or on other construction sites in town if he's lucky. There aren't so many girls in Gaspésie in the winter. He already misses Mary, tells himself that winter is going to be long. Mary didn't cry, or maybe she did, but just a little. She looked for Paspébiac on the map; she wondered if Bay des Chaleurs was really warm, if it was too hot, if maybe she could live down there. She is looking forward to the spring, hopes Patrick will return, but you never know if you'll see people again. You have to stop your heart from swelling too much with hope, you have to realize that sometimes "See you next year" is just "Goodbye, have a nice life" in disguise.

•

Cecilia has started school, Maata too. Cecilia has just started, while Maata hopes to finish this year, and maybe, if she is brave and strong enough, learn a trade, or learn something, anything, be able to talk about something too, say that Quebec City is beautiful, that it looks like Europe, know what Europe looks like.

Patrick has left, so Félix doesn't have to share the truck anymore. They're curled up together on the backseat, Félix's head on Maata's knees. She traces grooves on his back; she writes her name with her fingertips on his shoulder blades so that he remembers her, so that she stays in his skin. She knows the end is near.

"I wish I could go to Quebec City."

Félix smiles, says it's a really beautiful city. He tells her about the Plains of Abraham and the Château Frontenac, the river and Montmorency Falls, and Maata doesn't dare tell him that she doesn't care, that the most beautiful thing from Quebec City is lying on her knees and that he is what she wants, that the Bonhomme Carnaval can go fuck himself.

"Maybe I'll come see you in Quebec City."

He smiles, but says nothing.

33

YOU KNEW THAT SHE HAD SEEN him, but you didn't worry about it too much, you knew that he would be leaving very soon. You knew that she would be sad, that maybe she wouldn't sleep, or even eat, but you would take care of her, like you did before, you would take care of Cecilia too, she would see that you are the only one who really loves her, that you would never abandon her, not you.

You were ready to share her, let her have her fun in a white man's arms if that made her happy. You were ready to let her go if she promised to come back. You weren't mad at her anymore, your friends could make fun of you if they wanted but you would never touch a hair on Félix's head. You would do nothing to hurt Maata, even if the whole world was laughing at you behind your back.

He left before September ended. You found out because Maata got up early, went outside to the porch to watch the plane go over your heads, followed it with her eyes until it disappeared at the end of the sky before sitting down on the stairs and staying there, completely still, until Cecilia appeared, wearing her backpack, ready for school. Maata stroked her hair, watched her get on the yellow school bus. Cecilia loves the bus. Every morning is a celebration, getting onto the spunky old wreck. Maata wishes she could get on too, but the route stops only a few kilometres away, it never goes all the way to Deception Bay, much less all the way to Quebec City.

You made her breakfast. She didn't eat. She went back to bed. Timidly, you asked her if she was going to go to school today. She didn't answer. She was far away, in a luxurious bedroom in the Château Frontenac. Tenderly, you tucked her in.

34

ANNIE THOUGHT HER LIFE would get back to normal, peace and quiet, but peace never returned. Annie still couldn't sleep, wondering where he was, if he had gotten drunk, if he was hungry, if he had killed himself. She didn't dare call her cousin to check if Tayara had gone back to Salluit. She spent hours staring at the telephone, not knowing if she wanted it to ring or not, whether she was expecting good news or bad. And then it rang. It was the hospital. Tayara was in a horrible state, but he wasn't dead. He had been found early in the morning in the doorway of a Jean Coutu pharmacy, half conscious, his face covered in blood. He couldn't remember anything; he'd been drinking, of course.

Annie jumps into her car, talks to God as she drives, tells him: "Thank you, thank you for having saved him, thank you for having gotten him out of there, thank you, my lord, I didn't have the strength, forgive me, thank you, God, oh thank you." She runs through the maze of the hospital hallways, finds his room. He's sleeping. She sits in a chair and watches him sleep, watches his swollen face: "I'm sorry, God, I didn't want this to happen." She removes the chain with the crucifix from her neck and wraps it around Tayara's wrist. She prays: "Please God, give me strength." She prays for God's strength to oppose the destructive force of her people, of the men, of their collective suicide, in small doses, of the genocide that they are programmed to wreak upon themselves. She prays for hours.

35

THIS MORNING, MAATA THINKS she's going to be all right. She gets up and takes her shower. She gets Cecilia dressed; there aren't a lot of clean clothes left. She promises herself to do a wash in the evening. She thinks about how Halloween is coming soon. She'd like to sew a costume for Cecilia. She'll ask her mother to help her. She puts two bowls of cereal on the table, one for Cecilia and one for herself. Elijah is still asleep. She peels a banana. Its smell spreads, with a violence, through the kitchen. She lets it fall from her hands and runs to the bathroom. She barely has enough time to lift the lid of the toilet before she starts throwing up.

Cecilia skips over, contemplates her mother kneeling on the floor. She has seen her father and lots of other people in this position, but never her mother. Maata hugs her tight. She gets up, notices Elijah, who has been observing them from the hallway. She doesn't say anything, grabs her books and goes off to school. Elijah helps Cecilia with her coat and goes outside to wait for the bus with her.

"Why is Mummy sick?"

"It's her heart," Elijah says. "Her heart hurts."

The school bus arrives. Elijah tells Cecilia not to worry. He watches her climb on and wonders if his heart will also survive this, and his head. He thinks of the months that are coming, of the whole village still whispering behind his back: which one, which one, which one. He wonders the same thing.

36

TAYARA DIDN'T THINK HE'D BE coming back. At least not like this. He thought he'd come back on a private jet, covered in gold chains, real ones, massive gold chains hanging from his neck, a girl hanging from his arm—an American girl, a girl from Hollywood or L.A., a girl with grapefruit breasts and a tiny waist, and everyone would have been so jealous.

But he comes back the way he left, in the same plane with the same people, or almost; they're interchangeable. And he can't escape it, there are Sallumiut on board, distant relatives or kind-of-friends, and they all want to know everything, but he really doesn't feel like talking; his face says it all. He folds himself into a seat way at the back and puts his headphones on.

He finds a cousin at the airport, invites himself into her truck. She drives him to his place, asks him if he brought anything back to celebrate with, says she would love to come in and have a drink, but he doesn't have anything, nothing to drink, nothing to sell either, sorry.

It's after six but nothing is simmering on the stove. It smells like booze and his mother is passed out drunk on the sofa. It's just as well, he doesn't feel like talking. He locks himself in his room, eats the rest of the pizza that Annie bought him at the Trudeau Airport. He wonders how much time he has left before Aleisha comes and screams in his face or threatens him with a knife.

She arrives a little after midnight. He was almost asleep. She slams his bedroom door and dives onto his bed, jumps astride him and raises her right hand to give him a sharp slap, but then she notices his face and stops. She lets out a little shriek.

"Go ahead, hit me. It'll be nothing compared to the beating I already got."

She slides to his side, presses her body against his. "My poor sweetie, tell me everything." He doesn't want to, not now. He says he needs to rest. She kisses him but it hurts. "I'm sorry," she says, "I'm so sorry. Wait, I know what will help. Your balls aren't injured, are they?"

He closes his eyes while she gives him head, thinks about those black bitches in the videos, comes.

37

THE LAKE, THE DEAD LEAVES, the campfire that is crackling now because Laura felt like having one and so he made one, at ten in the morning. He found some old marshmallows in the back of a cabinet. She expressed doubts about whether it was a good idea to eat them, in the same tone that her mother would have used. Félix swallowed one whole, and they both burst out laughing. Then they roasted the rest.

Félix feels like eating marshmallows at ten in the morning, with wieners and potatoes cooked over the fire. Laura looks at her father and finds him handsome.

"How come you don't have a girlfriend?"

He doesn't know what to answer. He says that her mother still takes up too much space in his heart for him to let anyone else in. He thinks he has not loved another woman since Maude, and as he is saying this, somewhere thousands of kilometres away, a woman is thinking only about him, a woman watches the Canada geese fly south and dreams of following them, a woman who would simply alight, quivering, on the lake lapping the shore a few metres away from him. He wonders if, in a perfect world, he could ever love Maata. The women of the North never think about a perfect world, they love and that's all, no matter the distance, the skin colour, the language and the thousands of things that separate them; the men of the South see them like pretty pieces of furniture that just wouldn't go well with the rest of the things in their living room. Félix wonders if he could ever accommodate Maata somewhere in the cottage he has turned into a house. He doesn't know. Doesn't know if he would make Laura a little sister with blue almond eyes, doesn't know if the flowers of the tundra could grow in the South, doesn't know if both of their silences would end up being too much. He has never made plans for the future with anyone other than Maude; he doesn't see how he could start now. He has always preferred ephemeral girls, has always avoided the ones who wanted to set down roots. He feels like putting out the fire now and going inside, but he smiles at Laura and offers her another marshmallow.

38

FRIDAY NIGHT, VODKA at Steevie's. The house is full of people and smoke. You weren't that keen about going, but you also didn't feel like drinking alone at home while staring at Maata's belly.

Tayara enters the living room like a gold medal winner climbing onto the podium. Tayara the star player, the war hero, the local superstar gone to shine in Montreal, come back to recount his glorious adventures to his miserable little people. Aleisha stays next to him, hanging on his arm. She interrupts him at random moments to stick her tongue in his mouth and devour his lips, nip at his neck, wrap herself around him like a carnivorous plant.

And suddenly the royal couple notices your presence. Tayara forgets the story he had been starring in, Aleisha assumes the air of an outraged queen whose honour must be avenged, but you don't give a fuck; they don't scare you, neither of them do. You get up, you stand two inches away from Tayara's swollen face.

"You think you're so great, you think you're better than us, but you're a loser too. What amazing stuff did you actually get up to in Montreal? Nobody gives a fuck about you outside Salluit."

You took your time as you left the house. You didn't turn around or look over your shoulder. You knew he wouldn't touch you, because he's just a wimp, and because the wounds on his face could not take any more blows. You drank down the rest of your bottle as you walked home. You got on your quad and you sped up the mountain. You wanted to sleep at the camp; you were ready to freeze in the badly heated shack just for the luxury of not having to see the village when you woke up. You had headphones on and alcohol inside. You came up out of nowhere onto the road by the river, you never saw the truck that was coming down the hill. It burst your back wheel, your body tracing a perfect arc in the cold, dry October air. You crashed into the bottom of the pit and you thought to yourself that you had won, you would surely not see the village when you woke up, and then you fell into an icy sleep.

39

FOG. MAATA'S FACE. You want to touch it, but it escapes you.

Your mother is leaning over you, stroking your hair. There are knife marks on her face. She is smiling despite her bleeding gashes.

Cecilia. You don't know where she is; you want to ask if someone has seen her but your mouth won't open.

You are lying in a canoe, your gun on your shoulder, and you aim at a seal. The blood flows in the sea. You haul the beast into the boat. Your grandmother, sitting on the floor covered in old pieces of cardboard, cutting away the fat, scraping the skin. Your first seal.

They place your body on a stretcher but you don't see anything, you are far away, your canoe is floating swiftly towards the strait. They carefully immobilize you, but you aren't about to move; you are broken into a thousand crumbs and you aren't there, you have gone hunting. *Leave me alone, come back tomorrow, come back another day, I'm not there.*

You're all trussed up on a stretcher. A plane especially dispatched from Puvirnituq, *stench of rotten flesh my love,* comes down on the runway in the middle of the night. They haul you up inside like a seal in your canoe. The doctor fastens his seatbelt and the plane takes off again. There are two ways to get a free trip to Montreal: commit a crime or have an accident. The plane flies south as you dream of the tundra.

You open your eyes. Your whole body hurts. You can't move. You can't see the village. Just white walls. Ghosts. A science fiction movie, like the ones you sometimes watch. You wonder if you are dead. It's not like what you've been told. Liars. Blizzard. You can't see anything anymore, there's just this whiteness. You fall asleep. You're going to freeze to death.

Maata is sleeping as well. She had to wait until the next day to fly south. She hid in the back of the plane and she's sleeping, curled up into a ball. She is afraid to see an aunt or a cousin. She doesn't feel like explaining that Elijah is lying in shattered pieces at the hospital in town. Doesn't want to admit that a strange feeling is starting to replace her worry, doesn't want to confess that she is thinking even more about Félix than Elijah, that she hopes that nothing is seriously wrong with Elijah but also that she really hopes to see Félix again. I am a monster, she tells herself, I am a monster.

40

MAATA BLOWS ON ELIJAH'S FACE. She places a kiss on his forehead. Gets up, sits down again. She doesn't know what to do with her body. Her body aches, like Elijah's. She slides a trembling hand into the pocket of her jeans, closes her fingers around the slip of paper. That precious slip of paper. The phone number that she managed to wrench out of Rémi before her hurried departure for Montreal.

She leaves the room, wanders through the hospital looking for a public phone. She dials the number. He answers. She can't speak. She says she is in Montreal. He knows. Rémi told him. He says he feels so bad for Elijah. He asks how he is doing.

"He's all right. He's going to be all right."

She holds her breath. She asks if he can come see her. He says that Montreal is far, at least three hours by car; he says he is far away to Maata who has just come two thousand kilometres, who would have come on foot if she'd had to. He mentions his job, his daughter, his car, which has seen better days. He says, "I'll see." He says, "Okay." He says, "Tomorrow, I'll come tomorrow." Maata hangs up and collapses into a chair. She stays there for a long time until her legs are able to to carry her again. She goes back up to Elijah's room. She doesn't leave him, she keeps her eyes on him as though to excuse herself for inviting Félix to Montreal. She kneels by his side, she prays. The nurses exchange intrigued glances. They barely dare to move or speak for fear of breaking something, of precipitating their patient's death, as if it was Maata who was keeping him alive.

"Christ, it's like she's Saint Kateri Tekakwitha."

Maata doesn't falter, she keeps praying. Her lips move silently. When evening comes they tell her to go get something to eat, get some sleep, come back tomorrow. She eats something in the cafeteria, she doesn't know what. She goes back to the YMCA, paces around in her room, finally manages to take a shower. The next day she is not sure if she has slept, she doesn't know what time it is, but she gets dressed and returns to the hospital.

Elijah is awake, but that doesn't last long. He suffers less when he is asleep. She holds his hand. She sleeps too, a little, her head on his chest. Then suddenly she gets up like a startled caribou. Félix is there, hesitant and awkward in the doorway. She stands up and they gaze at each other, not knowing what to do. He holds out his arms, she runs to him and he hugs her. They hold their embrace for so long that it seems they will stay there like that forever. When the nurses come around, they are stunned, don't understand what is going on. They want to enter the room but don't dare disturb them.

Félix suggests finding somewhere else to chat, even if neither of them is very chatty. Maata follows him to the cafeteria. She tells him about the accident. He describes the duplex he is building, maybe his last contract before the winter. He talks about renovations he has got to do at his house, about the lake that is so beautiful this time of year with its autumn foliage, about how he needs to catch up with his daughter, who missed him all summer. He asks if she is going to stay long in Montreal, and she says, "No, just a few more days," and then she'll go back to look after her own daughter; Elijah should be able to follow in a few more weeks. He wishes her luck, he wants to go, and she says she would like to go to the lake when Elijah gets better. His gaze is tender, he strokes her cheek, he tells her that she has a man in her life who loves her very much and who needs her, a little girl who must be missing her mother.

"And what about you, do you love me?"

He says it's not simple, that they come from two very different worlds. She isn't listening anymore, it doesn't matter, he is saying thousands of sentences now which all mean no; she doesn't have to listen to each one. She has a tremendous longing to feel his arms around her, his prickly beard on her cheek, but she says goodbye to him and heads back to the room, biting her lips to stop herself from screaming that she might be carrying his child.

Félix gets back on the 40 going the opposite way. He feels like an asshole. So now he gets to add another girl to his collection of broken hearts, all because his own heart is inconsolable, he always does this, he always ends up destroying those of other people. He tells himself he ought to avoid women for the next twenty years: damage control.

He goes home. There is a message from Maude: "We have to talk. This is getting ridiculous, all this negative energy is bad for me while I'm pregnant. Please." He erases the message and opens a beer. He tells himself that maybe he should go back up north after all, so they would just stop bothering him. *Sorry ladies, but I am an asshole, I can't help it, you've been warned.*

41

WINTER HAS SETTLED IN. You glued all your pieces back together, Elijah. It was a slow convalescence in the polar cold, a winter cooped up in an overcrowded house, no long Ski-Doo rides to escape the crying kids and the family quarrels, months of painfully dragging yourself from the bed to the sofa on broken legs. "I'm broken, all broken, put me outside and let me freeze to death," you wailed at them one time, but that didn't last too long; soon you focussed on healing yourself with a fierce sort of patience.

Winter has settled in. Maata glued herself back together too, Cécilia's ear against her belly for hours, Cecilia watching for the smallest sign, the smallest message from her little sister, because she swore it was a little sister and never wavered. Maata spent the winter playing Mother Theresa; it did her good to take care of you, of Cecilia, and of the little one on her way, to religiously attend classes, to be a wife, a mother and a model student. It did her good, it kept her from thinking of other stuff.

Winter is long where you live, but it does end. May is milder, the cold stings less and the geese come back, announcing their return like idiots; all you have to do is pick them off. You insisted on going hunting, and you brought back three. You felt happy for the first time in months.

And at the same time as the geese, the construction guys return. You wondered if he would come back. With a little luck, he wouldn't and the village would gradually forget that he had ever existed and would stop believing that you might not be the father, once again.

42
"Rémi!"

Rémi turns around to see who has called his name, with such joy in his voice. It's Félix, freshly off the plane. He threw his bag on his bed and flew back to the kitchen, anxious and excited as a kid who doesn't know yet whether he will be in the same class as his best friend. They are both happy; they catch up on everything that has happened in the last few months, they promise each other they'll go fishing. Félix reveals he has brought a bottle of white wine to go with the mussels; they can hardly wait. Félix looks around the room, finally asks if the girls still work there.

"Mary does, she should be here tomorrow. Maata doesn't, she... can't right now."

Félix asks why. Rémi hesitates.

"She's pregnant. She should be having her baby in a few

weeks. And, um, Félix. I don't know anything about pregnant women or babies, but you should know there are rumours going around. People are saying, they think... Because of the dates and all that, some people put two and two together and it's none of their business, but they figure that..."

Rémi can't finish his sentence, but Félix understands. He shakes his head. He returns to his room, puts on his coat and goes for a walk. He walks towards the road that will go all the way to the mine one day. He can't take it anymore. What gets into these women, to have babies all the time? He accepted this contract so that he wouldn't have to hear about Maude's baby and now they want to put another one in his arms. He doesn't want any babies. *Leave me the fuck alone, for the love of Christ.*

43

MARY DOESN'T KNOW how she'll manage to get through to the end of the meal, until the dishes, how she'll be able to stop herself from spilling everything onto the floor, breaking all the plates; her heart is leaping uncontrollably in her chest. He's back, her Patrick is back, all smiley and shy, stammering as he invited her to go for a ride in the truck after the meal. He'd been afraid of losing his place. Really? How ridiculous. Come on!

The men finish eating. Mary manages to wash their dishes despite Rémi's teasing, which makes her even clumsier. Old Peeta, who is replacing Maata, gently pulls her tea towel from her hands. "Go on, dear. I'll finish up." She flies to the parking lot and almost knocks down Félix, who is going out for his walk. He waves to her but she doesn't wave back. That will teach him to hurt her friend Maata. Patrick starts the engine as soon as he sees her. He doesn't dare kiss her, not yet. He waits until they are hidden from view, on the road. Then he holds her face as he kisses her as if it were made of porcelain, and Mary whispers, "You're back, you're back, you're back." Later they return, happy in the bright May evening light; they are driving by Maata's house. Mary asks Patrick to stop, she darts up the stairs, goes in without knocking, and calls to her friend, who arrives in the vestibule with the slowness of a woman about to give birth.

"Félix is back. Did you know?"

No, she didn't know. Mary tenderly strokes her friend's cheek. She doesn't say a word, because there is nothing to say. Maata watches her go outside and join Patrick in the truck. They kiss right in front of her house. She turns her back on them and drops into a chair.

She wonders how it's done, how a heart can heal, how to stop trembling and continue to hope, even now. It's not fair, she did her best all winter to forget him, to devote herself to her family, to love Elijah and stop dreaming of Félix; she did her best but the wall she built around her heart begins to crumble the moment he sets foot back in the village. It's not fair.

.

Maata can't sleep that night, and in the morning she doesn't feel like going to school. What's the use of getting exhausted trying to make something of your life if everything just breaks down thanks to one guy? Cecilia comes to snuggle next to her and this gives her the energy to get up. She walks to school. Félix, fixing up a house across the street, spots her as she goes by. His eyes cannot peel themselves away from the material of her coat, stretched to the max over her lovely round belly. His legs go soft. He is relieved to be inside. He moves away from the window to make sure she can't see him.

"Hey Félix, isn't that your Inuit? Well, look at that. Seems like she's gonna have a little one pretty soon. Would that be a little Félix, by any chance?"

He bursts out laughing, happy as a pig rolling in manure. Félix drops his tools, grabs him violently by the collar and flattens him against the wall. He can vaguely hear the other guys trying to calm him down, but he just feels like hitting, hitting hard. He remembers his daughter and manages to hold back. He picks up his tools again. He doesn't say a word to anyone for the rest of the day.

He tells himself, *I'm not just an asshole, I'm a violent asshole. What is happening to me?* He tells himself he would be better off leaving this place, maybe go somewhere deep in the tundra. He could build a little camp, like others have, and just stay there, not see anyone anymore and forget himself too, if he can manage to.

44

She was born the 12th of June, early in the morning, luminous like a spring sun that never quits, and Maata said that she was yours. You were happy and you also wanted to cry. You carefully held the baby's head against you, Maata's head in the hollow of your shoulder. You Inuit, you make these children, magnificent, just dazzlingly beautiful children, as marvellous and stunning as an Arctic summer solstice. You came from far away and you have known death, but your survival instinct is strong, and you produce magnificent children.

You asked Maata if the little one could be named Eva. Maata smiled; you kept rocking her with infinite tenderness, this tiny Eva, and it occurred to you that the spring thaw would be less painful this year, that you wouldn't need to go looking for ghosts in the fjord anymore, that life had just given you an incredible chance.

.

Summer gently settled in. Maata enjoyed going for walks carrying Eva in the hood of her coat. She was lucky to be born in the summer, not have to face the rigours of winter right away.

Maata walks along the river's edge. She thinks she recognizes the silhouette that is coming towards her, but for the first time, she doesn't feel an earthquake in her belly. Yes, it's Félix. He looks at her timidly. She stops and faces him.

"Hello Félix. This is Eva."

Félix leans towards the baby in Maata's hood, strokes her face, her little hands. It's been a long time since he's seen anything so beautiful. He wishes he could speak, but he can't. Maata takes his hand.

"It's all right. Okay? It's all right."

Félix nods. He squeezes Maata's hand very hard. He lets her go. He knows he will never see her again.

Some people said she wasn't yours, Elijah. We'll never know if they were right, like most of the time, here. Anyway, they belong to the whole village, these children.

ACKNOWLEDGEMENTS

Thank you to my family for all your love and unfailing support and for sharing this dream with me; Jean Désy, my wonderful mentor, for his passion, insights and "old geezer" advice; l'Union des écrivaines et écrivains du Québec, for their fantastic mentorship program; Frédérique Dubois, my very first reader, for her great sensitivity, patience and care; Frédérick Lavoie for his sharp eyes and for the encouraging words which managed to overcome all my doubts; Mélanie Laurendeau, Geta Etorolopiaq, Aipilie Napaartuk, Levina Puttayuk and the residents of Module du Nord for the correction of my Inuttitut; Gerry Delaquis and Catherine Cyr-Wright for the logistical support which allowed me to keep writing when my computer let me down deep in the bush, in Haiti; the team at La Peuplade, for their generous, attentive and passionate way of doing things; my Inuit friends and all the lovers of the North who shared their stories with me: Qujalivunga.

Thank you to Anita Anand, my translator, for her natural rendering of my voice into English; and finally to the folks at Véhicule Press for their enthusiasm and trust, and most of all, for taking *Nirliit* on this new adventure.

ESPLANADE
Books

THE FICTION IMPRINT AT VÉHICULE PRESS

A House by the Sea : A novel by Sikeena Karmali
A Short Journey by Car : Stories by Liam Durcan
Seventeen Tomatoes : Tales from Kashmir : Stories by Jaspreet Singh
Garbage Head : A novel by Christopher Willard
The Rent Collector : A novel by B. Glen Rotchin
Dead Man's Float : A novel by Nicholas Maes
Optique : Stories by Clayton Bailey
Out of Cleveland : Stories by Lolette Kuby
Pardon Our Monsters : Stories by Andrew Hood
Chef : A novel by Jaspreet Singh
Orfeo : A novel by Hans-Jürgen Greif
[Translated from the French by Fred A. Reed]
Anna's Shadow : A novel by David Manicom
Sundre : A novel by Christopher Willard
Animals : A novel by Don LePan
Writing Personals : A novel by Lolette Kuby
Niko : A novel by Dimitri Nasrallah
Stopping for Strangers : Stories by Daniel Griffin
The Love Monster: A novel by Missy Marston
A Message for the Emperor : A novel by Mark Frutkin
New Tab : A novel by Guillaume Morissette
Swing in the House : Stories by Anita Anand
Breathing Lessons : A novel by Andy Sinclair
Ex-Yu : Stories by Josip Novakovich

The Goddess of Fireflies : A novel by Geneviève Pettersen
[Translated from the French by Neil Smith]
All That Sang : A novella by Lydia Perović
Hungary-Hollywood Express : A novel by Éric Plamondon
[Translated from the French by Dimitri Nasrallah]
English is Not a Magic Language : A novel by Jacques Poulin
[Translated from the French by Sheila Fischman]
Tumbleweed : Stories by Josip Novakovich
A Three-Tiered Pastel Dream : Stories by Lesley Trites
Sun of a Distant Land : A novel by David Bouchet
[Translated from the French by Claire Holden Rothman]
The Original Face : A novel by Guillaume Morissette
The Bleeds : A novel by Dimitri Nasrallah
The Deserters : A novel by Pamela Mulloy
Nirliit : A novel by Juliana Léveillé-Trudel
[Translated from the French by Anita Anand]

LIBRARY AND ARCHIVES CANADA CATALOGUING IN PUBLICATION

Léveillé-Trudel, Juliana, 1985-
[Nirliit. English]
Nirliit / Juliana Léveillé-Trudel ; translated by Anita Anand.

Translation of: Nirliit.
Issued in print and electronic formats.
ISBN 978-1-55065-494-3 (softcover) – ISBN 978-1-55065-501-8 (HTML)

I. Anand, Anita, 1962-, translator II. Title. III. Title: Nirliit. English.

PS8623.E9444N5713 2018   C843'.6   C2018-900696-X
C2018-900697-8